The Spark Before The Flame®

Brenden Horned

Preface & Gratitude

This book is dedicated to those who want to grow into a better version of themselves. It is important to look back at where you were in order to find where you want to be. However, remind yourself of where you are going and do not dwell on what has happened, simply grow from it.

I would like to thank those who have only seen the best in me and provided me with the tools to be who I am today. A special thank you to my family, friends, past, future girlfriends, and even people who may not like me. Without you, I would not have experienced what fortunate events have taken place in my life so far. I am very grateful for those of you who are taking the time to read my book as well. I hope that you find something useful in this book and find it exciting to imagine.

The characters in this book are fictional and do not represent any person. Some of the events that take place in the book resemble events in my life, but the book is fictional.

I would lastly like to thank those on my team who have helped me to achieve this publication.

The Spark Before the Flame

Brenden Horned

©2021, Brenden Horned

Self-Published

Email: brenden.horned@gmail.com

Table of Contents

Music & Social

I wanted this book to be different than any others I have read. So I decided to create a folder of playlists you can listen to while you read the book. The songs in these playlists relate to how I wanted the different chapters to feel. Every song was picked by myself, Brenden Horned. Some songs may be explicit and all credit is given to the artists of each song.

Spotify

Amazon Music

Spotify-
https://open.spotify.com/playlist/3AzOMh6Us8bpALpniyjygI

Amazon-
https://music.amazon.com/user-playlists/dbc378a414ea454baae8e83472e1608asune?marketplaceId=ATVPDKIKX0DER&musicTerritory=US

Instagram

Facebook

Prologue

Spotify Prologue Playlist

https://open.spotify.com/playlist/0IllzTP9S2wI68kD6IZty0

Amazon Prologue Playlist

https://music.amazon.com/user-playlists/f10d160f0d7545e8be1639666262d4
c8sune?marketplaceId=ATVPDKIKX0DER&musicTerritory=US

Prologue

My name is Desmond, I am 19 years old and now I reside in Seattle, Washington. I have learned so much within the past 19 years, but there are two specific moments that stand more prominent than the rest. When I fell in love for the first time and then when my first love left me. This is who I am and who I loved.

First you should know me. I was fortunate enough to grow up in a healthy household with two brothers and a sister. My sister and I never truly connected as well as my brothers and I. Nevertheless, we still had a mutual love for one another that we hated to admit. We were family, and no relationship troubles would change that. My brothers and I had been close, but not until recent years did we grow closer. I had switched schools many times before graduating, but I did not mind. Finding friends was never difficult for me as long as I was looking in the right place.

As for sports or grades, I was proficient in neither. I was good at English; however, sports or good grades never really came easily to me. I had attempted track, swim, basketball, and soccer but I was good at none of them. I had never truly dedicated myself to sports or to my education in all honesty. Instead, I would watch all of those unrealistic movies where the perfect man would come along and make that one special person happy. As sappy as that sounds, I admired that and sought to become that man. So I found myself willing to truly dedicate myself to becoming this type of man, just like in the movies.

I began with chivalry, if nothing else, I would prove it to be very much alive. This was much more simple to learn as my parents had already raised me to respect others to the best of my ability. I am very thankful they did because I would never wish to hurt someone as I and many others have been hurt. But that is for another time.

My appearance was borderline insulting to fashion. I had always been lazy in how I dressed, as I had no intention of impressing anyone. Now that needed to change, this was no easy task, as it truly took me at least a few years to find a style that fit me. I had tried everything in between blue jeans, t-shirt, and a hat all the way to beanies, khakis, and a peacoat. I was raised in the country so I was the only one who had clothes like that at school. My friends would question and often joke about my clothes at times, but I knew there were people that liked how I stood out from the rest.

I also began searching for a sensible taste in music, which proved difficult given that I grew up in the country. Often my father would listen to country music and my mother to Christian music. Country music was all my small town in Missouri listened to and it quickly became overplayed to me. I went through an EDM and heavy metal phase before I began listening to many other genres. I started listening to R&B, pop, alternative, and even some classical. I had learned that music was an art form and not every great piece of art is created using the same method.

Chapter 1

Spotify Chapter 1 Playlist

https://open.spotify.com/playlist/7bekae9HCGO7i2DSrVkAM1

Amazon Chapter 1 Playlist

https://music.amazon.com/user-playlists/40e1b2fecfa84d4d9b5c3ba2212e14f
csune?marketplaceId=ATVPDKIKX0DER&musicTerritory=US

Chapter 1
Desmond Allen Clermont

My full name is Desmond Allen Clermont and the names of my siblings are Julius, Gideon, and Jesebelle. I never really cared much for my middle name, I thought it was bland and boring. I am truly in no position to complain though, given my unique first name. Everyone in my family was fortunate enough to have unique names that stood from the crowd. Jesebelle is the oldest and I am the youngest of all of the siblings.

I am now the tallest in my family standing at 5'9", but when this story begins I was only the second tallest as Julius held the title. I have blonde hair and blue-grey eyes that are sensitive to sunlight, every girl's dream right? Not really, they cared almost as much as atheists care about Passover. I was never really fond of my bright blonde hair, thankfully as I grew older it became darker.

I was a terrible child growing up, I lacked patience and cared for school very little. Both of my parents had explicit rules during my childhood, but a large portion of them were fair. They raised me to understand that the world is difficult and painful. I first went to a private school an hour away from where I lived and it was one of the most difficult schools I have ever been to. I then was switched to a much closer private school which lacked organization and formality, so I was pulled from that school as well. I then made an effort toward online school, to which I had no accountability. After my parents had enough, they finally sent me to public school for 9-12th grade.

Public school helped greatly with my social skills and I enjoyed learning the way other people think. I had changed so much by late freshman year. I was no longer the country, soft, oblivious boy, but I was a firm, kind, and sweet young adult. I began to work out right before my freshman year because I had been incredibly short and somewhat chubby throughout middle school. I never saw much progress until senior year but I was still much better than before.

I was good friends with only a few people at that time, they were fun to be around, but rarely ever serious about anything. I had a girlfriend named Allie and I considered Allie my friend; however, we rarely saw each other unless it was at school. I grew somewhat sad when I was with her because I feared that every relationship was like this. I had always dreamed of romance like I had seen on tv and read in books, but we had nothing like it.

When I was attending virtual school, I was in a very despairing place. I had no car to leave the house to see anyone and honestly, I had nobody to see. Most of my friends were left behind at private school and I was home on a farm without anyone to talk to. I became very sad and felt myself and my mind withering away each day I was isolated. That was when I started to work at the community center and make new friends. I was getting better but even when I went to public school I still didn't feel whole.

From 7th grade to the end of freshman year I was always acting out and getting into trouble. I had so much anger and sadness built up that I didn't care what was right or wrong. Although I have always been a mother's boy, I am close with my father as well. He typically lets me have more freedom. I am incredibly thankful for everything my parents have done for me, even though they were strict at times, it paid off.

I was close with my grandmother on my mother's side. She used to pick me up from private school and would help me with my math. She would always feed me and make a punch for the two of us. My grandfather was in the army and is a very stubborn man but my grandmother knew how to put him in his place. My grandfather had his own chair parallel to my grandmother's and I would always sit on the couch as we watched tv. It was very bonding to have such loving grandparents at the time, even my grandmother on my father's side was always loving toward me.

I still remember the day my mother got a call and as I peered over at her, she told me to put my shoes on. My maternal grandmother was in the hospital for a long time. She had contracted an infection from an open wound. They knew when it was almost her time and snuck me into the ICU to see her with the rest of my family. I will never forget when my uncle Drake asked me if I wanted to hold her hand and I said no. I was young and scared, I thought that maybe if I didn't hold her hand and accept the inevitable, then maybe she wouldn't have to go. Ever since then I regret saying no, and I hope that she knows how much I cared for her even though I was too afraid to show her.

I now know that I will never make the same mistake twice. I sought out to trust myself more and become more confident. I thought for a while that maybe my dedication to reach all of these goals was just to distract me from the pain and sadness that once surrounded me. Either way, I was still determined to become the guy that girls would love to have. I know that sounds wrong and conceited but I wanted to be better than I was.

I had already changed so much from where I first began but I was still not anywhere close to where I wanted to be. Then before I could continue to improve any more, I met her.

Chapter 2

Spotify Chapter 2 Playlist

https://open.spotify.com/playlist/1yN6XRLeaJqQ8yAnRvTDm4

Amazon Chapter 2 Playlist

https://music.amazon.com/user-playlists/144cfcefa2454a1a857b0d464d4420ddsune?marketplaceId=ATVPDKIKX0DER&musicTerritory=US

Chapter 2
The Voice

It was cold, the air was dry, and the grass was frosted white from the previous night's dew. I lived a great distance from where I worked at the time, but I had stayed the night with a friend of mine. We were both recently sixteen and had stayed up very late the previous night. I got a call that morning, and I did not recognize the number or the voice that sounded through the phone. I quickly realized I had forgotten to set my alarm the night before and was late to supervise lifeguards at the pool I worked at. Luckily, my friend Paige lived across the street from the pool. I told the voice on the phone I would be there soon. I scrambled out of bed, threw on my work uniform, and put a warm coat on before sprinting out of the door.

It was a community center with an indoor pool, and I had just walked through the doors into the humid air before noticing her. I had worked with her once before, but she was new on staff. I instantly knew it was her remarkable voice that woke me that frigid morning. After quickly setting my things in my office, I walked over to the side of the hot tub where she waited politely with the chemical testing kit. I acted as if I did not care that she was there. Yet that was not true, for some reason I did care, I cared very much. I had no reason to care, I had worked with very attractive girls before and was truly unfazed. There was just something about the way her face glistened in the humid sunlight that drew me in, it is quite scary to think of how she did it. We quickly tested the chemicals together, I then headed back to fill out my paperwork. We were not the only two working, but I barely spoke with the other employees that day as I was under some kind of spell set by the girl whose voice echoed over the phone.

I remember I had looked into her hazel eyes and found it nearly impossible to look away, they were soft, warm, and endless. I felt pure happiness and joy running through my still body when I saw her happy, it was like she injected pure bliss through my veins with only a look. I knew it was wrong to feel this way about her because I had a girlfriend at the time. But Allie was a high school crush, I was learning about myself, I would not call it love. I thought that simply as an excuse for how I felt for the girl I worked alongside.

There was also another issue, is dating a coworker okay or even allowed? I was determined to find out but I knew I would never be able to cheat, it was not in me to do that to a person. I was borderline obsessed with the girl with the voice on the phone, and the way she made me feel completely limitless and light. The minute I got to my office alone, I skipped through each page of the schedule looking for one single name, line by line.

It became hard to focus on anything, she was on my mind constantly and involved herself in every minuscule thing I did. Even when shopping I would walk by something and wonder if she would wear it or use it, should I get it for her? I had barely known her, I hadn't the slightest clue as to whether she even liked me back.

I was worried with how I felt for her, it was dangerous for me to feel this way for someone when I needed to focus on bettering myself. She had made me feel like I was already more than good enough and I was afraid I would give up on my goals. So I halted everything and shoved my feelings for her as far down as I possibly could. I continued to hang out with Allie which was wrong, but it was secure and safe. It worked for a moment but I continued to think of the girl with the voice. I knew I had to do something, anything to feel this way all the time.

Allie's focus was not school work and she was a bit rough around the edges. Unlike a lot of girls our age, clothes and her appearance didn't matter to her. She was very swept up in the high school experience. She was also oblivious at times, but she excelled at sports. As I think of it, we weren't very similar at all and saw each other very little. Looking back it seems as though we had truly brought out the worst in each other, but we were both happy to be cared for. The girl with the voice had no clue at the time that I had a girlfriend, but I cared little because I still had no idea if she held the same fascination for me as I did for her.

The following week we worked together again. One of our co-workers pulled me to the side to tell me they noticed the way we acted around each other and hoped the fun, carefree atmosphere continued. However, they also told me she had a boyfriend. I let out a sigh and hesitated before thanking and assuring them nothing was going on between the two of us. In that moment I could feel a pit forming in the middle of my chest and I still had no idea who this girl really was that I was so strongly drawn to. I knew I was a fool for thinking I was good enough or that she might feel the same way for me.

Yet I still had a difficult time focusing, not because I thought of her, but because the pit that formed in my chest felt so real. I was sure I was going to be okay, but I was unsure as to when that would be, how much longer must these feelings last? As I began to focus on myself more and get back on track with the things I had previously been working on, I heard it. It was her name. The sound of her name caused everything that had been submerged in the darkness of the pit to resurface.

I wanted to rid my thoughts of her, that girl with the voice on the phone, and continue my pursuit of a better me. My longing for her was more complex, it was more than attraction, it was passion and happiness. I was so caught up in her I had lost track of every moving part in my life. Even hearing her name gave me chills, her name caused the hairs on my neck to rise.

Chapter 3

Spotify Chapter 3 Playlist

https://open.spotify.com/playlist/1rdqBxRs9ukLYTrbDw9PKP

Amazon Chapter 3 Playlist

https://music.amazon.com/user-playlists/476547a87c3540be916bad2d265558
6dsune?marketplaceId=ATVPDKIKX0DER&musicTerritory=US

Chapter 3
Ella

Her name was Ella, Ella Dallas West. The name that rang through my head constantly with no remorse for the damage done to my thoughts. Every word she had ever said to me played on repeat during all hours of the day and night. I was incapable of holding it within me any longer, I had to finish things with Allie, it was unfair to her. I met with Allie before school began and told her of how I had learned so much from her and was thankful for her but I knew that we were not right for each other.

Immediately I felt a sense of relief, I no longer felt guilty for how I perceived Ella. Now I was only bound by the feelings I had for Ella, whom I eventually began to call Ell. We began to work with each other more, and every day we did I learned something new about her. Her favorite color was purple, and her favorite flower was a white rose. It had been slightly over a week since she delivered my wake-up call and I was aching to call her mine.

She had a boyfriend and I knew this, but I had to know more about her. Every night I thought of what I learned about her. I began to make excuses again, it was okay that we hang out platonically, right? I worked with her that Tuesday and we talked about our favorite places to eat. I was excited because she liked sushi too! We were cleaning the storage room together and I remember she tripped and grabbed a hold of my arm to catch her fall. Her eyes looked up at me and we stood silent for a moment as if a spark had been struck between us, the kind of spark that only ever happens before a flame.

We left the storage room and I swallowed my nerves long enough to ask if she would like to go get sushi with me, just as friends. Before I was able to respond to her answer my heart had dropped and I couldn't find my breath. She had told me that she couldn't because she had homework, but I knew that wasn't true, it had to be the boyfriend.

My body ached for the rest of the day as I distracted myself with work and later made dinner.

As I pulled plates from the cabinet I heard my phone sound a ping, it was Ella. "Hey, I didn't mean I would never hang out with you, I just have a lot of stuff to do tonight." I finally felt my heart return to my body and responded "Oh yeah of course, when are you free this week?" She told me Friday, so we planned to meet at 5 pm at the community center.

I was filled with both excitement and worry. Everything I did to be the better me I felt wasn't enough. I waited until she pulled into the parking lot in her little red truck. I quickly jumped from the seat of my car to greet her. I said hello and hugged her with firm closed arms that quickly let go before I opened the car door for her. She looked ravishing and smelled of flowers, it was incredibly difficult to focus on the road when every one of my senses was drawn to her. "Where are we going to eat? I'm starving", she said as she got comfortable in the passenger seat of my 2000 Pontiac Grand Am. I asked her if she had ever been to a restaurant by the name of Longboards, she shook her head no. "Great!" I said, it was perfect for friends casually hanging out together. We could order a Hawaiian wrap or bowl and simply talk to each other.

We arrived at the restaurant and talked as we waited for our order to arrive. Even after we got our food, we talked about everything, it was perfect. She told me how she was truly unhappy with her boyfriend and she had been waiting to leave him in fear of what he might do. I sympathized with her, but fireworks erupted from my stomach, was I what she was waiting for? At times we would be so close to each other I could almost feel her breath on my lips, I liked that. We finished our food and I opened the door to leave so I could take her to our next destination.

There was something about the drive to the 24/7 store near us that was so peaceful and full of joy. When we arrived neither of us made any move to get out of the car, we were talking about her sister and how she questioned Ella about me. Once the cool air had settled in the car, we finally walked through the doors and looked at every section of the store piece by piece. We had made it to the home decor portion of the store and I asked her if she had a wall carpet (that is what I refer to tapestry as). Her hands quickly covered her chest as she began to laugh, but not a laugh I had ever heard before. This laugh was loud and constantly breaking, but for some reason I felt as though I wanted to hear that laugh every day for the rest of my life.

We began our journey back home but the mood had changed drastically. We both knew that we would wake the next day without the other and go on waiting till the next time we could see each other. Maybe that was wrong to say given she had a boyfriend, even though we had both thought it. As we parted ways I told her to call me once she had arrived at home so I knew she was safe. I meant that, but I also needed to hear her voice once more before I slept.

So just as I asked, she called. She called me that night, and the next, and two days after that. Three or four days had gone by since our first adventure. I enjoy writing so I read her a story I had written for a class about a girl. "Who did you write this about?" she asked, "I wrote this for someone we both know and we both see often". She asked if it was a coworker, but I finally told her it was her.

Just as the silence became uncomfortable she told me she had left her boyfriend. My heart raced as it never had before and I stumbled to find words. "I'm sorry to hear that, but I need to tell you that I like you... a lot." I could hear a smile appear through the phone before she sighed and said "Well, I like you a lot too Desmond."

Chapter 4

Spotify Chapter 4 Playlist

https://open.spotify.com/playlist/3ZY24aOJlxOMz5xQtxrZDQ

Amazon Chapter 4 Playlist

https://music.amazon.com/user-playlists/c56e33a1da6841ea8500383ac00875
81sune?marketplaceId=ATVPDKIKX0DER&musicTerritory=US

Chapter 4
The Fire that Grew

Ella was on my mind constantly and the possibilities of what could happen next played over in my head like a broken record. We were finally free to express our feelings for each other without guilt. We began texting constantly the following two days, it was simple and lighthearted. Three days after we expressed our feelings for each other we planned to meet, but time began to move much more slowly. Though I felt somewhat guilty about Allie, I was determined to not let that emotion affect my future with Ella.

It was finally the third day and I was trying my best to act calm, but truthfully I was terrified of ruining what felt like the start of something great. Once I arrived at her house, I knocked and as she opened the door I heard her father ask me to enter. As I did so, he questioned me and made polite jokes. I was then much more comfortable and managed to respond with humor. He appreciated that and he chuckled that he liked me before sending us on our way. She had asked me before today where we would go and I told her it was a surprise and she would have to wait. Truthfully, I had no clue what we were going to do and I liked that, it felt weightless.

We began driving, but we weren't driving to a destination, we were driving to see where we would end up. I had never been able to do this with anyone before and it was blissful. We were driving through a small town not far from hers when I stopped. I remembered there was a beautiful park hidden behind a hotel nearby that was full of color. As we walked through we noticed a wedding was in service and we joined them for a moment before they all went inside. A few people looked at us quizzically, wondering if we should be there, but the ceremony was nearly finished so they let us play along. After they had all gone inside the hotel we took pictures in the gazebo that held the wedding. Ella was beautiful, she glowed bright enough to light the moon at dusk.

Every moment I spent with her I felt utterly complete and whole as if she was what I had been missing my whole life. This was dangerous, I had given up on improving myself because she made me feel like I was already enough. The ancient Greeks believed that each human had double of everything, two heads, four arms, four legs. Zeus feared their power so he split them in two, condemning the separate halves to find their match. I am Christian, but could I have truly found the one or is this feeling going to hurt me? Either way for some reason I wasn't afraid, quite the opposite, I was excited to discover what would happen next. Every time I saw her I felt like she was all I needed to survive in this cruel and cold world.

In the park I hugged her, looked into her eyes, and whispered gingerly, "Ella Dallas West, will you go out with me?" her smile grew to lengths I had not yet seen, she then let out a giggle and responded, "I would love to Desmond".

That very moment had previously played over in my head a hundred times, but never just the way it happened. The way it happened almost seemed better than the hundred outcomes that I had imagined. I was vulnerable with her because I felt like she made me stronger than I was before. I know that the human heart doesn't have much to do with emotion, but it did feel like after I met her every beat of my heart was meant for her. She became everything I had ever wanted before I could even blink. She would often pout as if she was a child and it was quite charming. But she was independent, if there was a mountain that she needed to climb, she would do it alone. Everything she did wrong only made me want her so much more, her wrongs wouldn't upset me but let me know she was human too.

We worked together the day following our first date and I remember the way she looked at me when she walked through the pool doors. That very moment continues to play over in my head now to haunt me in her absence. Working with her was different, it was hard to focus on other people or paperwork when there was someone right outside my office that had taken my world and made something entirely new of it.

Even from the doorway of my office I could hear others whispering about us. I did wish they would mind their own business but "Ella and Desmond" did sound good when said together. Besides myself and Ella, the only other thing anyone had talked about that day was the fact that it was snowing. I tell everyone that I hate Christmas and winter in general, but that is not completely true. I do hate the stress of money, family visiting, and the possibility of wrecking your car, yet I do think it is one of the most beautiful times of the year. I loved to see the city right after the roads had been cleared and the clouds flowed over the nearly vacant street. I only ever told people I hated this season because I have never been able to show or experience it with another that I was utterly in love with. She was open about her love for this season and Christmas, I admired that about her and wished I had that appreciation.

There was something about the cold that made the touch of another human so much warmer.

Ella was loved by her coworkers. She was truly adorable and a very kind person. Although she seemed very popular, I soon realized she was quite shy and avoided conflict. She told me a personal story of how she was once popular at school but someone spread lies about her and she changed. I liked the person that she was though, I liked that she would hang out with people that would never be "popular" and made them feel perfect as they are.

I soon realized she was very smart and had great goals in life that set her apart from anyone else. She wanted to be a doctor and save people's lives. She was also great with kids and wanted to be a good mother. Another goal of hers was to travel when she was older and could afford to. We learned something new about each other constantly and it seemed as though we would never know enough about each other. The way she talked about things that she loved or her goals gave me one of the purest forms of happiness I have ever experienced.

So weeks continued full of adventures and dates as we craved the presence of each other more and more. After a month had passed, on a Wednesday, we were able to see each other yet again outside of work. I picked her up from her house, once more with no real plan but to be close to each other. As usual, I opened the car door for her and ensured she had settled herself in the passenger seat before we moved toward whatever lay ahead of us. Spring had quickly appeared and the weather was becoming warmer. We didn't want to go far, so we stayed in the small town in which she lived. First, we went to a park where we only sat on the bench, but it was everything I wanted because she was there.

It was the first warm day of the year and we drove to the local ice cream shop. We chose our flavors and went to my car. We talked even more, but this time her eyes seemed deeper than they ever had been. The only thing that kept me from falling helplessly into her sublime hazel eyes was her lips that appeared to slow down time. She began to speak softly, and as I mirrored her tone it seemed as though we grew closer inch by inch. After looking at her soft, full lips that she began to play with, I looked into her eyes once more. Feeling her breath warm my lips, still sticky from the vanilla ice cream, we kissed. Her lips were just soft as they connected with mine and refused to separate, when they did it was only for a second to catch a breath. I could feel the sparks once again in the pit of my stomach as I sank my tongue ever so slightly between her lips only to meet hers. This continued for another moment before we released our latches on each other and looked in awe of what had just occurred. We both knew this changed things completely, yet we weren't afraid, but utterly prepared for what was to come next.

We had to leave each other shortly after that, but we were never fully without each other that night. I could still taste her vanilla ice cream and soft, sticky lips when I arrived at my house to call her. We began to call every single night. That night when we called, we were both struck by the way time stood still. The kiss that lasted only seconds was in fact closer to fifteen minutes.

To others, it seemed as though we saw each other a healthy amount between work, adventures, and calling every night. For us it was never enough time together, every hour seemed like a mere ten minutes. We had both discussed whether we would tell our friends of our recent developments. We promised each other to only tell one person, but we both knew that it would be more than that. It is difficult to keep something inside that runs rabid through your mind constantly.

We were happy; I was happy and felt complete for once. Had I finally worked hard enough on my own improvement that it allowed me to finally find the one for me? Time and further discussion will reveal the truth about this question, but it didn't matter because there was no way I would return to working on myself for me. Now I could only work on improving myself for her and what she needed in her future. This wasn't about just any girl anymore, it was only about her.

We worked the next day and were nearing the end of our shift. "Hey handsome", I turned my head to find Ella edging closer to me with an irresistible smile. I had promised her we would have dinner after work together and I could see the hunger on her face as she approached. Though I wasn't able to tell from her eager face whether she was hungry for another kiss or dinner. "I've been working up an appetite all day, where are you taking me?" I wondered if we were talking about food or something else? No matter, we decided to go to a restaurant nearby.

We sat down, myself after her, and ordered our drinks. She was wearing a blue tank top, black leggings, and a purple Nike hat. She ordered a steak and I ordered a burger. I recall waiting for our food as she explained music theory to me on a napkin. I had no idea what she was talking about, but the look on her face and how she talked with such energy made me smile. I tried to confuse her on what she was saying, and I did for some time before she looked at me and softly burst out "RARW, STOP IT." she growled at me often and it was quite possibly my favorite of all her adorable mannerisms.

We didn't see each other again until that next Saturday; we planned to meet at work in the early afternoon. I waited a moment for her to settle into the passenger seat once again, but this time was different. Once in, she kicked off her shoes and put her feet on my dash as if she now owned that side of my car. "Excuse me, ma'am, what is this?" I asked her with a grin. She then responded with a clearly artificial upset face "My shoes hurt, are we going or what?" I then drove off to our destination just south of us.

We first went to Longboards and the store once more to reminisce about our date as "friends". I then took her back to her bright old red truck and helped her over. She asked me to follow her back to her house and we would finish our date there. Her dad was going to be at a concert all night and her sister was staying with a friend. As I shook my head yes, she remarked in glee "I'll race you there!" I looked into her endless hazel eyes and replied, "What's wrong with taking our time?" She sat in her truck in complete silence for a second before I kissed her quickly and entered my car. The mood had instantly changed.

I followed her to her house, but the moment we arrived she received a call from her sister. Her sister needed to be picked up from her friend's house. I could tell she was slightly upset as the tension between us only grew in moments like these. We obliged and picked her sister up. She didn't like me at the time. There was no real reason, she just really liked Ella's ex-boyfriend before me. Once we picked her up and dropped her off, Ella and I went to the store. We had no intention of buying anything, we simply wanted to find trouble. Between racing bikes around the store and playing with the hula hoops we were infrangible. Other relationships looked up to us in admiration because we weren't afraid of anything other than having to leave each other at the end of the day.

The sun began to set and we drove south to a field where we watched the sunset in my car wrapped in each other's arms. Once it had grown dark we left for ice cream. Shortly after, I dropped her off at her house as we ended yet another adventure. Our lives quickly became molded together, we would go on adventure after adventure, it would never be enough time together.

Yet another month had gone by and I had bought a promise ring she admired without her noticing and I then drove her to the park we went to when we first hung out. I brought her to the gazebo and looked into her eyes as they sucked me in further with every gaze. "I know we are young and we haven't been together for very long, but every minute I am with you I am happy and full of joy. Now that I know what it's like to be with you I don't want to be without you. Ella Dallas West, I am completely and utterly in love with you..." her eyes widened almost in sync with her smile before she let a giggle of happiness slip. She then pinched her lips and replied, "Desmond Allen Clermont, I am completely and utterly in love with you". Just as my smile began to grow, our lips met like they never had before. Full of passion and desire they refused to release unless it was to let out a laugh of happiness.

Sushi, ice cream, and adventures became our new normal, it was everything I had wanted but didn't know where to find. The desire that began the day we picked up her sister had only grown bigger and stronger and it became more difficult to resist the taste of her or the heat from our bodies together. We had not yet been fully intimate as I was a virgin and she had only had sex once.

A few weeks since our declarations of love for each other we had yet another day full of adventures. As the night overcame the day, we picked up takeout for a night picnic. Once we ate, we laid on our backs with an alluring view of the stars scattered across the black sky. We talked for a long time and our voices noticeably became more quiet and soft. I began to watch her gazing up at the stars before she looked back at me and our heartbeats began to sync. Just as we closed our eyes, we pulled each other in closer and closer to fill the gap between our bodies. Every kiss and pull made the desire between us even stronger until it was irresistible. I unwrapped her clothes just to trace a map on her flawless skin. Every moment was powerful, intimate, and full of emotion that only made us want each other more. I had always seen her as something to nurture, but now a part of me saw her as something to dominate.

Our ideas of each other had changed completely. I was no longer her innocent and polite boy, she began to see me as a strong, intimate, and forceful man. Just as I no longer saw her as my innocent and frivolous girl, she was now a ravishing and risqué woman. This did not tarnish my love for her, rather it grew for the way we encased our every feeling in each other. It was like nothing I had experienced before. That moment ran through our heads every night for the next week. This only verified what we had was more than infatuation and more than mutual attraction. As if she hadn't taken control over my world already she quickly became a drug, she was my new addiction.

Chapter 5

Spotify Chapter 5 Playlist

https://open.spotify.com/playlist/02DVfNHXis4hxoxTmfbh8M

Amazon Chapter 5 Playlist

https://music.amazon.com/user-playlists/144a81995bd94b158987e413a362d
7fesune?marketplaceId=ATVPDKIKX0DER&musicTerritory=US

Chapter 5
My Life Reborn

I have always considered my life a story or a movie and this was a new chapter. Everything fell into place just as it should have and I felt complete whenever she was nearby. I always thought that it's a little deranged, but it could be possible that she was my gift for all those years of unhappiness. We couldn't even bear to think of goodbyes, so they became until next times. Truthfully, the next time never came soon enough for me.

We had more adventures over the following months and she got to meet my whole family, even those that lived on the west coast. I met her entire family and we did everything we possibly could together, which made my daily tasks so much more special.

I got in trouble quite often until I met her. She showed me how to have fun without breaking the rules. Something as simple as going to the store or for a walk would often become the highlight of my day with her. She showed me enjoyment in safety just as I showed her fun in danger. I learned to balance the danger and safety in my life so that I would never become dull or banal. I looked at my life in joy instead of hatred and disgust, it was all because of her.

Her homecoming was edging around the corner and I knew she deserved to be asked out in an astounding way. I was lazy waiting until the last minute, then I dashed between stores to come up with ideas and buy supplies. I created the sign the night before and told her to meet me at the community center. I had left a scavenger hunt around the building that led her to me holding the sign asking her to be my date to the dance. She was embarrassed by the crowd that surrounded us but right then, I made her feel like the princess she was.

Later that evening after we went to the city to shop we met a friend of ours, Calum. We worked with him and would hang out with him often. Calum was funny, but he struggled with appreciating himself. Truthfully when he first began working at the pool, I did not like him and saw him as a threat to my relationship. Ella pleaded for me to give him a chance, I did, and we quickly became friends. When caught in my short times of despair I would still fear he may jeopardize my relationship with Ella. That night the three of us went for a drive and simply teased each other. It was very liberating just enjoying the company of each other. At the end of the night, Ella quickly kissed me excited for the dance the following week.

Her family wanted pictures of us together before we ventured to the dance, so I met them at her house. I remember my heart racing through every corner of her living room as I waited for her to finish preparing. I was talking to her dad, but the minute she walked into the room my throat closed up. So many words were fumbling through my head that I couldn't choose just one. So instead I smiled and stood up to admire every inch of beauty beaming in front of me. Her dress was navy blue with a flower-stitched bottom and straps that rested to the side of her perfectly bare shoulders. Throughout the night I could not keep my eyes off her as every movement dragged me back into her astounding presence.

The dance was fun, her ex-boyfriend held a pretty significant grudge against us, but nothing that concerned us. Her friends grew fond of me and I wanted to make sure I gave Ell the best night she's ever had. I had taught myself to slow dance properly for this very moment and it was so magical we could feel the stares of other people bounce off our skin. I also sadly recall doing other dances that caused me to be a hot topic for the next few school days. I was glad Ell's friends were impressed because she deserved to have a boyfriend she could be proud of.

In all honesty, she was completely out of my league at that time and I was fortunate to have her. However, our relationship was never perfect. We did argue and get upset with each other more often than I mention. I was slightly terrified to have something so precious and incredible, so I did begin to start fights over useless topics. I grew very protective and needy as I wanted to see her in my future for as long as possible. I know that I am a jealous and protective person. We live in a world where we have little control. So if there is something that I love, I will protect it at all costs. I see anyone who seeks to take what I love from me as a threat.

I feared being compared to the other men my age because I saw myself as a product. There was a need and I yearned to be the option that everyone wanted. This was likely where my love of business was created and grew from. But I was more than a product, I had feelings and needs from those who wanted me. She was what I wanted and I had normalized her. I normalized the attention and love that she gave me, not understanding how much of a blessing it was.

Aside from cheating, one of the worst things you can do in a relationship is normalize being with that one person. By normalizing them you get used to your life with them, not realizing there could be a time you no longer have them. It is important not to be controlled by them but still cherish them. If they control you, then you lose all control yourself. They should cherish you just the same as you do them. If they don't, then you must make yourself valuable to them. I had no intention of seeing myself single again after I had told Ell that I loved her. I gave her what she wanted and took what I wanted from her expecting no consequence.

Our fights that seemed to become more and more common didn't seem to hinder our love for one another. She loved the world without a thought of hatred and that was one of the things I loved about her. I did my best to protect her from the cruelness it had to offer. When I couldn't I would hold her hand and pull her to the warmth and safety of my arms. Concerts, adventures, or walks in the city, the world seemingly harmonized to us. It had been over a year and the only thing that still gave me pure bliss was to see her smile in glee.

Every part of my body ached for her, she became my world and I completely accepted it without a thought. The way she looked at me she... she would never leave me, we do everything together. Except work together.

I quit my job at the community center that fall, due to disagreements with the management staff. I had already secured another job as a server at a restaurant 45 miles from my house. Truthfully they had taken advantage of me and my position as if it was not necessary, so I had to leave. This was very difficult for our relationship because we saw each other most at work and we were not used to this much distance. It was a challenge to get similar schedules so that we were able to see each other enough.

It was different between us after I left that job, but we were still Desmond and Ella. We were still happy, passionate, full of adventures, and intimate with each other. Everything shifted, but we still were able to harmonize with the world and set our own boundaries. Every party, vacation, or adventure wasn't complete until I looked in her deep amber eyes only to see what I wanted for my future. We still argued at times, but we only did this to better understand each other and our feelings. I remember we would always playfully argue about who would break up with who. She had always insisted I would end up leaving her and I assured her the opposite. The only difference was there was something deep inside of me that always felt she would leave me and only one of us was right.

I remember that every night I felt like my life was surreal or I was surrounded by staggering beauty, I would look at her. Something about her full smile or endless amber eyes kept me grounded to earth as if she was my gravity to this world. Everyone at some point wins and loses in life, but every second I was in her presence I was winning. I dreamt of her every night and on the days I spent with her, I was never sure I woke up. We were complete aside from my jealousy and unnecessary arguments, which continued.

One night specifically stands out in my memory because of the rush of emotions I felt. It was late and I was on the phone with Ell for one of our typical nightly calls. We both grew tired after sharing miscellaneous events that happened throughout our day. Her ex-boyfriend had talked to her that day. Aside from asking her how she was, he had told her she looked good and that he wanted her back. This left me infuriated. Why does he feel he can speak to her after breaking her into pieces? I picked those pieces up and worked endlessly to place them correctly together so she was able to grow. Now he feels entitled to try his turn again? I was utterly livid by this. I had been having a peculiar sensation in my chest that became more common each month. She knew of these episodes and had told me to alert my parents, though I would not because I thought they were just a fluke. My anger from what he had told Ell caused an episode that would change my life forever.

Chapter 6

Spotify Chapter 6 Playlist

https://open.spotify.com/playlist/2PDwUYvF2YrD8TYdhRKF3o

Amazon Chapter 6 Playlist

https://music.amazon.com/user-playlists/689da1f1deda4109b08bb069e573c0
0csune?marketplaceId=ATVPDKIKX0DER&musicTerritory=US

Chapter 6

A Broken Heart

I remember the sensation of my chest pulsating rapidly to the point I could not lay still. The first time this happened was months ago at work with Ella. I laid down and began to stabilize before they called an ambulance and after they alerted my parents. Ell drove me home that night, which was completely out of her way. Once we arrived I was much better and my parents sat me down as my mother held the hand that Ell was not. I was exhausted and my entire arm was still shaking discreetly. I went to bed and I didn't think of the episode until the night I was on the phone with Ell. I never knew that episode would be the beginning of something that would affect me forever.

I was brimming with anger, but it went away quickly once I began to feel the same rapid thumping in my chest. I began to stutter and mispronounce words. It became impossible to sit still or speak. Ell knew when I began to stutter that something was wrong and she continued to call my name, each time her voice breaking more. At this point it was at its worst because I couldn't sit still, it became hard to breathe and all I could hear was Ell screaming my name through her tears. I was full of pain, fear, sadness, and remorse for Ell having to experience what was happening to me. I could finally start to breathe again and felt my body fall into a set state. Everything returned to normal, but now I had this burning pain in my chest.

After this, I felt like I had been run over by a truck at 100 miles per hour. My body was sore, my chest in pain, and my eyes heavy from exhaustion. With what breath was returned to my lungs, I comforted Ella. She screamed in frustration demanding that I tell my parents and I assured her I would. After I comforted her and she began to wipe her tears, my voice became soft and hoarse yearning for rest. She stayed on the phone with me that night until she knew I was asleep and comfortable. I vaguely remember that just as I fell asleep a voice told me I was safe now. It was reassuring, but this wasn't the voice of Ella or myself.

I was still hesitant to inform my parents of these episodes because I knew that my life would be different after that. I could tell anytime that a simple symptom appeared around Ell that she was scared and upset. My hands had always been as cold as ice due to their lack of blood flow. But it was different now when I brushed my hand against her cheek to wipe the worry from her face. She would typically find some warmth that pulsed through my arctic hand, but now she jolted her face away from my frigid bloodlessness.

I told my parents the very next day of my episodes because I never wanted to see the pain that I saw on Ell's face ever again. We booked an appointment to meet with our family doctor in two weeks. I was excited to tell Ell that I made an appointment and that she didn't have to worry anymore. My doctor ordered tests that I completed, then all we had to do was wait for the results. Each week the doctor ordered new tests but the results seemed to show nothing of interest. One week I had to wear a monitor on my chest that recorded my heart 24/7. The results from the monitor finally showed some abnormality, but the doctor refused to see it as abnormal. After that, we switched doctors who ordered different tests each week.

Prom was here and we had something to distract us from our arguments, we were happy again. We were excited to have a stress-free night full of nothing but each other in our purest forms. It was Saturday, April 13, 2019, when I was sitting in her living room once again, just like I had during Homecoming. She was announced just before she walked from what seemed to be heaven itself. Her purple dress, riddled with jewels that fit to her waist then flared, only brought out the beauty she already possessed. I choked on words just awaiting them to spill from my open mouth as I fell in love with her once again. I refused to take my eyes off of her the rest of the day in fear I would forget something so beautiful was directly in front of me.

Things began to change rapidly after a magical night of affection, beauty, and pleasure. My test results had come back and I went to an assigned cardiologist on April 23. During our meeting with the doctor, I could almost feel an episode coming on as I zoned out. They noticed my loss of attention and they hooked me up to a machine as an episode began. It was clear I was calm but struggling to control my body as it began to jerk in every way it saw necessary. My doctor decided to admit me into the hospital for the night to track my episodes. They began to occur more and more often.

In my hospital room, I was helped to get more comfortable by a volunteer. It was a girl I had previously gone to school with. I used to have a crush on her as she was very beautiful, but she was not what I needed right then. I needed to be healthy and warmed by the touch of Ella lying next to me. Our communications were cut slim due to my episodes and constant visits from different doctors. That night I had one more severe episode that left me weak and worn.

The next day a group of cardiologists came into my room and explained that I suffer from Postural Orthostatic Tachycardia Syndrome. This meant that my heart rate would race because of my change in posture, sickness, or even when I am in pain. They also said that my uncontrollable shaking and loss of blood flow was likely just a panic attack from the feeling of my disease. I was irritated and embarrassed that they thought it was anxiety, I was never one to be anxious. Had they taken the time to get to know me they would have realized I am a very relaxed person.

They had told me they were going to discharge me that afternoon after one more doctor, a neurologist, saw me. Before the doctor was able to visit I could feel yet another episode preparing to erupt. My parents were frustrated that they were going to discharge me before I was even slightly better so they recorded me. This episode continued to worsen, I vividly remember the uncontrollable shaking and pain. Tachycardia is when your heart rate is above 100 bpm, my heart rate at that moment was over 200 bpm. I was trying to control my breathing with no results as my parents comforted me from each side of my bed. I was scared and felt as though it was possible that I could die. Everything began to darken and my body tingled just before my heart rate dropped.

The neurologist had finally arrived and after a few simple tests and watching the video recorded of me, she had an answer. She said she had seen symptoms like this before in similar patients and it was a simple fix of one over-the-counter medicine. There was simply a bubble of air in my throat that was pressing against my autonomic nerve causing more severe symptoms. This worsened my POTS symptoms and caused more severe episodes.

This was a relief and we were very happy, but this was not the first time that I was in the hospital for this. The last time was slightly less severe but I did wish Ella would have been there for me. She offered once and I told her she didn't have to, but a portion of me only wanted her by my side. At the time I didn't consider how scared she must have been. Just as I was when standing at my grandmother's bedside, she was scared. I was scared too, terrified. There was a moment in the hospital during an episode where I began to feel myself passing out. It didn't feel like passing out, it felt as though I was drifting away unsure as to whether I would return. I knew it would work out, but a piece of me wondered if I would live through the episode. Ell and I talked that day but things were different, I could tell just from the way she seemed distant.

I was homebound after this, she came to my house a few times and I drained every inch of love from her that I could. I kept her close so I didn't have to worry about being without her as much. I think there were times when she wanted to argue with me but she felt sympathetic for what I had been through so she just let out a sigh while motioning for distance between us. This by no means was our end, I was getting better and able to go out into the world once more.

May 4, 2019, we went to a local festival in her small town and I remember during the parade I took a picture with the clown just to see her smile and hear her euphonious giggle. Her laugh echoed throughout the space only to bring attention to the most lively and likely embarrassed beauty on the block. The morning of June 19 we cooked breakfast together listening to music, her french toast continues to make my mouth water. And on October 21 she had a choir concert and I was grinning because I imagined the others were singing just to impress Ella.

Time was hurting us and we both realized that. We were working a lot and we had a lot of responsibility set by our families to ensure our future was successful. We had dreamed of forever but that's all it was, a dream.

Sunday, November 17, around 9 pm, I was locking up at the restaurant and called Ella on my way home. I was tired and upset, all while she was cold and bitter. I pondered over whether I had done something to hurt her.

"What happened Ell, why do you hate me?" I questioned. "I don't hate you, I just don't know" she responded with frustration spilling through her voice. "You don't know what? Whether you love me anymore... Do you still love me, Ella?" I exclaimed but was scared to hear a return. "I... I don't know," she said. I'm not sure my brain could attempt to comprehend what she meant.

I asked her if she still loved me, thinking I already knew the answer. This was just another fight among our many that we had in the past two years of our lives together. My mouth was as dry as a desert, likely because all of the fluid in my body was flowing to my brain in order to process what was occurring. I was holding the water that urged to pour from my eyes back, only to continuously tell myself that it was just another simple fight. This was just going to be a lonely night but I will be fine, she will surely come around in due time.

I did not call her the rest of the night, I simply drove home with the music at low volume so that I was able to hear myself think. The drive seemed endless and desolate, there was nobody anywhere in sight. This was likely because it was late that night, but at that moment it seemed like the whole world knew I was not to be bothered. Once I arrived home I simply sat in my car in complete silence for a few moments before I found the strength to go inside.

We had not broken up, this was just a pause where we would spend time away from each other only to realize we needed each other. While I thought this, I texted her letting her know that I was home safe and I hope she found her way home okay as well. I expected a response, anything to assure me that we would be able to figure this out. I waited first minutes, then hours until my eyes were sealed by the burning of restlessness. One thing that had always truly bothered me was going to sleep upset with each other.

I awoke the next day with still no response so I got ready and went to school. I was different, my friends would mention Ella throughout the day, but I didn't tell them we were taking a break because it was only temporary. Each class period seemed to last so much longer than any other day and there was nothing to ease my mind from the thought of her. It was difficult to resist telling anyone about my situation with Ell because of how much she meant to me. I was so full of emotions that I didn't want to show, so I just shut them off. I felt every emotion entirely, but I showed nothing while I was sanctioned in the unjust building of forced education.

Once the final bell rang I walked down the hallway with an emotionless but not yet despairing face, looking to the floor the whole way. Though I was looking down I could feel the quick yet heavy glares right before most of the students cleared a way for me. Once I arrived at my car and threw my bag behind the driver's seat, I began debating whether or not I should call her.

Something about that day showed me that I did not want to have to handle that amount of despair again. I called her and my heart dropped to the floor the moment that she did not answer. I had not had any big symptoms since I had left the hospital until now. It was slight, but it was there. I was now required to take 12 pills a day at the age of 17, but they helped, I was better so I complied. I drove home this time attempting to drown my thoughts out with my music at a dangerously loud volume.

I texted her too much and called her more than I should have but I hated every day that I had to wait. After a few days she had finally answered and I attempted to convince her to go for lunch so that we could talk about this. She refused and continued to make excuses that I simply couldn't refute because it would only hurt my position. After that conversation, the silence had continued and it was already reaching the end of the week. I thought I recalled her telling me that she worked that Friday and I was with Paige, the very friend I was with when her voice sounded over my phone for the first time.

I told Paige that I loved Ella and hated to feel this way, while he did his best to help me move on. I should have listened to him, but I couldn't just give up! I went to the store where I printed some of our favorite pictures together and bought a bouquet of her favorite flowers, white roses. Paige was then supportive and hopeful as well, so we rushed over to the community center right before she got off. As we waited I wrote a note on the back of one of the pictures that explained how empty I had felt during this time apart from each other.

I saw a familiar truck pull up that I stared at for a moment before I recognized who it belonged to. Its owner was someone I saw as a friend not long ago, it was Calum. We had recently stopped talking and I then knew my instincts about him were correct. I was worried at first but pushed that aside as I saw her come out of the building in a straight direction to her car. I met her there and I could see her frustration as I approached.

"Ella, I am still not sure if I did something to cause this but listen and understand I want you in my future and will do whatever is necessary to make that happen." She quickly responded "Des, what are you doing here? You shouldn't be here." Hurt by her words I mumbled, "I got you these and there is a message on the back of this picture but wait to read it... I see that our friend is here." She snapped "thank you, but you need to go home, go home now!"

I walked back to my car with thoughts racing so rapidly through my head that it hurt. The very second I got into the car I slammed my fists against the steering wheel in rage and continued until I ran out of breath. I waited a while longer in the parking lot, just long enough to see her get into the truck with Calum. Things changed and I knew Paige was right, it was no longer Ella and Desmond against the world. She was gone for good and what hurt the most was not being able to call her and tell her how terrible my day had been. I was not hers just as she was no longer mine, from then on our lives would not be intermixed. She was undoubtedly gone...

Chapter 7

Spotify Chapter 7 Playlist

https://open.spotify.com/playlist/011Pp2iYDFnKAO7KQCULvp

Amazon Chapter 7 Playlist

https://music.amazon.com/user-playlists/387a4ab7e19642edaba6e29a531e55b3sune?marketplaceId=ATVPDKIKX0DER&musicTerritory=US

Chapter 7
A Broken Heart Part 2

The next morning I awoke to my alarm sounding only to bring me into the world that now felt so empty. I wanted to call her, text her, hear the voice that sounded over my phone two years prior. Instead, I helped my parents with whatever they needed without complaint. I was angry inside that I volunteered myself for this, but I knew this was the only way to block what happened the previous night from slipping through my restless thoughts. I repeatedly assured myself that I was better off alone, but no part of me believed it. It is true you know... you don't realize what you have until it's gone. Everyone is guilty of taking many things for granted, I was used to the love that she provided and now I felt I needed it to survive.

I had what I wanted but I didn't enjoy the happiness she provided because I was so focused on what else I could obtain. I was also so very remorseful for a thought that I had while I was still with Ella. A few months before we broke up I remember thinking that I wanted to marry her one day, but I had hoped we would break up only for a little bit just so that we would be able to explore other relationships. This was wrong of me to think and not tell her how I felt. How would I even begin to tell her if I wasn't sure I meant it?

The next day I was driving to work telling myself I was okay as I let tears slip from my glossy eyes. I am a man and we hide our feelings, but there was nobody to see me as I let myself feel. Once the tears that I hadn't wiped dried, I grabbed my things and walked into work without showing emotion. It was painful to keep this up, I relied on tips and I might not get paid well due to my moodiness. I continuously went to the restroom and the breakroom to escape the people around me, to loosen the tight rein on my feelings.

I worked diligently to not look at mirrors during this time, I was ashamed. The person who looked back at me in the mirror was miserable and seemingly not good enough. After a breakup people believe that their ex-girlfriend represents all women when not wanting them, even I fell guilty to this misconception. My shift ended and now I didn't want to leave because then I would have to feel again. It seemed like everything she improved within me came falling down right before my face.

It is peculiar all the little details you remember when someone exits your life, things you wouldn't have thought about if they were still there. I remember the feeling of her hair caught in my fingers, the feeling of her breath on my lips, and even the warmth of her hand wrapped around my upper arm. I remember all the places that we went together, the different foods we tried, I even remember the different tone in her voice when she lied. I wondered if I should have slow danced with her amid the rain that one night below the stars because now that's all I see. I wished I had one more dance, one more kiss, just one more hug because now I would know not to let go.

She was once my everything but now she was simply a stranger who knew all of my secrets and insecurities. I found her in everything that I did. My memory of her yearned to ruin me. I would look at things and wonder if she would like it, or if she would laugh at a joke I thought of. I was lost without her, lost in only what I remembered of her.

She was not dead, but her ghost did haunt me, people began to look and act like her. Truthfully they were never really like her, I was just looking for her in other people so I could fill the void she left me with.

I had finally talked with other people and most were surprised by our breakup, but Ella insisted it was a slow decline. So now I was supposed to be free, but instead, I was bound by the thought of her. How could I have not possibly seen it happening? Was I never supposed to have that form of beauty? Thoughts flowed continuously which made it very difficult to stay focused on what was happening around me. She taught me how to appreciate myself, but I was appreciating myself through her eyes. I knew that if she asked for help from me I would comply because she was still such a large part of my life.

My friends told me I would get over her and I knew it was true but a specific thought kept cycling through my mind. "It was said that cells replace themselves every 7 years, but that's not completely true. After 5 days the cells in my stomach regrew not knowing the butterflies you gave me. Once 8 days had passed my lungs no longer knew what it was like to breathe the same air as you. After 14 days my skin cells died and I forgot the feeling of your hand brushing against my cheek. But the lens cells last a lifetime and I never forgot the sight of you glowing more than the stars did on the night of our first adventure."

When we were together my life had a rhythm, it wasn't mundane but rather safe. The fear of the unknown secretly resides in every human and we have come to terms with it. Every day began to blend together, all bound by the emptiness she left me with in the parking lot of the community center.

I went to school the following Monday and my friends quickly noticed something was off with me. They asked and I obliged, sparing emotion as I told them exactly what had happened over the past week. They apologized and offered to help in any way, but nothing would change the past. There was one specific friend that I had when I first came to school, but we had fallen away from each other for a bit. She was gone a semester of the previous year and I was gone prior to the breakup because of my heart issues. Her name was Angelina and we had 8th period together at the time.

I had talked to her about all of the adventures I went on with Ella and my feelings. She listened and enjoyed my stories of being a hopeless romantic in the modern world. Once I had told Angelina what had happened I could feel the hope in humankind dissipate from her soul. Astonished, she apologized and did her best to amuse me with the thought of finding someone better than Ella. I made jokes about our breakup only to cope and assist with the pain I felt within.

Have you been in love? Did they leave you? I understand that two years is nothing compared to many relationships, but two years is enough to become a part of one another. In four days you can fly around the world and within two years you can fly to Mars and back. In those two years of my life, I learned to appreciate the beauty in the world and found someone that made me better. I attempted to communicate and set up a lunch meeting with Ella but had no luck. Truthfully if she happened to say yes I'm not sure what I would say that I hadn't already said. What do you tell someone to change the way that they feel about you?

I would go to school, go to work, go home and visit with family, then go to bed only to repeat the next day. She took what spark we had and that took a part of me. When I looked in the mirror I saw a stranger I didn't recognize.

If I could find my way back, I wondered if she thought of the same things I did after we had broken up. "Ella, you fucked me up and changed the way I look at the world, at love. But I need to know, when you drive by that lake or pass our favorite restaurant do you think of me?" I said to myself in my car with the raindrops singing to my words.

My life continued to grow very monotonous, almost repetitive. Wake up, go back to when we were happy. I wondered if I would have done things differently or if I would have found a way to keep her. Our pictures haunted me but they were just some of the little things I had left of her. Our friends became her friends, but that didn't bother me because for some reason I was still worried with how she was doing. Then all I could see when I looked at our pictures was the history of what was and likely will never be again. It upset me seeing her smile when I looked back at what was. I had never been easily disturbed before she appeared in my life.

A part of me never left that parking lot when she told me to go home. I was standing still in that parking lot ever since while the whole world passed around me. I remember I used to love eye contact and everything that could be said just by looking in one's eyes. But she stripped that from me and took it with her when she left me. I couldn't bear to look into another's eyes out of fear that I would see the very eyes that I loved, the eyes that broke me. As I stood there, those that passed by me would bump into me and I looked to the ground in fear of falling down once again but with nobody to catch me this time.

Chapter 8

Spotify Chapter 8 Playlist

https://open.spotify.com/playlist/3ki8Tz3N7CiQofWwPBe2Ph

Amazon Chapter 8 Playlist

https://music.amazon.com/user-playlists/d8dddcb045b24703b3f0f564377f90
dfsune?marketplaceId=ATVPDKIKX0DER&musicTerritory=US

Chapter 8

An April Night

A few weeks had passed since the breakup and I remember I was at work when I received a notification. I waited and checked my phone once I entered my car after work that night. It was April, I had previously worked with her at another job before she went to college in Nebraska. I had always found her very smart and pretty but I was taken and never saw her outside of work. I was surprised that she had texted me. That night was the first night I had smiled in weeks and sincerely meant it.

We talked for a while that night and I was excited to see how she was doing. I was still constantly thinking about Ella, pondering what would happen in my life next? Nevertheless, after talking for a few hours April had told me that she was coming back to town for a few days. I asked if she would want to hang out one of the days while she is in town, she agreed. We decided on a Wednesday night after I got off of work at 9:00 PM.

My coworkers were astonished because I had entered work in a better mood than what had become typical of me. It was difficult to work knowing I would get to see an old friend soon. Once it was nearing our time to meet she came to my work and sat in my section of the restaurant. She looked beautiful... I began to lose my words and I continuously looked in her direction as I finished serving my tables. I came up to greet her and sat in front of her with a smile that had been lost for a long time. I told her I was almost finished and would change in my car before we left.

As I entered the kitchen doors, I told my coworkers about her and how we are going to the city that night. They looked at her and told me she was beautiful as if I had not known that already, but I simply agreed. I wrapped things up and headed to my car to quickly change. Just as I pulled my black dress pants down I saw her already beginning to walk toward my car. As immediate fear flowed through my veins, I rushed to put my jeans on and switch shirts. She arrived at my locked door just as I was putting my shirt on and embarrassment shadowed over her red face. I unlocked the car and she got in, letting out an adorable yet quiet "BRRR".

I started a playlist from my phone and we began heading toward the City of Fountains, Kansas City. It was simple, we talked about anything and everything that crossed our minds. There was no obligation and it was serene, almost magical. We both began to stare off at the Christmas lights as we drove by the Country Club Plaza, a popular sightseeing destination, but I preferred looking at April to catch a glimpse of her under those warm lights.

I parked and we started our adventure into the cool lively night to find a place for us to eat. We noticed many restaurants were closed due to the late hour of the night we arrived. So we explored a shop or two until we stumbled across a coffee shop. We got coffee and found a table where we sat for at least an hour talking with each other. I still thought of Ella that night but she wasn't on my mind at that time. Instead, I looked into April's eyes and could swear I saw the part of me that had gone missing for so long.

Once our cups had been emptied, I walked her to the door before opening it for her. As if it was an instinct, I gently held my hand on her lower back as she walked through the door. She looked at me through the corner of her eye as if I surprised her with this, but she only slightly hesitated before walking from my hand. I wondered if she was happy or if she felt my frigid, bloodless hand through the threads of her coat. Yet, the look that beamed from the side of her eyes confessed comfort.

Once we reached my car we both stumbled in and settled into the cold air waiting for the car to warm. We drove to a local spot I knew that had a great view of the Christmas lights. On the way she mentioned a songwriter she liked and without missing a step I handed her my phone with a motion to play them. She looked at me for a moment as if she did not understand or was not used to this. She began to play a familiar song that rang through my car in harmony. She sang, and I watched her. She was a music major and her voice against the one playing over the speakers left me in awe.

When we drove home we asked questions here and there but we mainly listened to music and sang together. I was not a good singer but any voice put in comparison to hers would be put to shame, so I sang anyway. We were weightless and every moment we grew closer to ending the night we became more silent. So many thoughts were flowing through my unsettled mind in regards to how I felt about her. "She is going to college a million miles away, I know long-distance doesn't work. It doesn't matter whether I like her or not, it will not end how I want it to."

Once we arrived at her car, we finished listening to the songs she had queued on my phone. The last few that we sang together I really enjoyed and I wasn't sure if it was because they involved her or because they were good. I walked her to her car and resisted every muscle telling me to kiss her, and instead only hugged her. She was warm and smelled sweet of cinnamon and spices. The air grew much colder as she left my arms. I told her to text me when she arrived home so I knew she was safe.

I left in the direction of my brother's house and listened to the songs she had just played for me on repeat. I arrived at Julius's house and he asked about April. I explained the situation and how I don't do long-distance relationships. He sat for a moment in thought but did not offer advice. Instead, we made food and found a movie to watch. He knew that there was no way to settle a mind restless over a woman. I went to sleep that night thinking of Ella but I somehow dreamt of April.

I woke up the following morning at peace, I thought of both April and Ella throughout the day. But there was a simplicity about being alone with my thoughts that left me eager. It could very well just have been hope from the night before. I could not say that I loved April because it was one simple date, but if anything, she restored my faith in one's addiction to another. I had been surrounded in darkness since the breakup because that part of me was still in that parking lot hoping she still loved me. The darkness was not gone but rather quieted by the thoughts of the previous night.

I drove home and enjoyed what bliss was available to me because I knew that even this comfort wouldn't last forever.

On Monday I went to school and awaited the last period of the day so I could explain it all to Angelina. I did just that with a subtle smirk laid across my otherwise settled face. She was happy at first but very disappointed in my lack of action toward a relationship with April. I was also slightly disappointed in myself, I knew we wouldn't have worked out long-distance, right? Was it possible my disbelief in long-distance relationships caused me to lose an opportunity? That didn't matter as I felt the darkness of Ella creep inside of me once again. It seemed as though in the absence of April, my thoughts of Ella continued.

That night I was texting a marvelous girl I worked with. She was beautiful and her personality made me happy even when I didn't necessarily want to be. That's how I knew she would be the perfect person to talk to, so we messaged for a few hours back and forth. It worked, I was happy and there was a certain feeling that she gave me that felt unique. I asked her if she wanted to hang out on Friday. She said yes and a smile that was lost until recently grew from one cheek on my face to the other.

The following day after school I worked with her and I greeted her with a painfully awkward "Hey". Once a coworker close in age with us figured out about our plans, she came to me. "Are you going on a date with her?" she questioned with joy in her voice. "I never called it a date, she doesn't like me like that and I only ask someone out in person" I responded. Her smile grew as she quietly exclaimed "I just asked her and she told me she wished it was a date, so ask her out!" I hesitated before nodding and walking to greet my new table.

I saw her later when neither of us had anything to do and we stared at each other. A tile had shifted in our attitudes toward each other. When we looked at each other it was only us two, and every moment it grew more difficult to look away from one another. Once I did break eye contact we both smiled and I looked once more into her eyes with intensity. I then asked, "Rose, what will we do on this date of ours?"

Chapter 9

Spotify Chapter 9 Playlist

https://open.spotify.com/playlist/2PFF7BjtnK7ctPw2cbCqsz

Amazon Chapter 9 Playlist

https://music.amazon.com/user-playlists/6d24fff6492d45d58298b423a9b810
83sune?marketplaceId=ATVPDKIKX0DER&musicTerritory=US

Chapter 9

A Rose Among Sunflowers

Rose was just that, delicate and beautiful. Along with those attributes was her smile that showered your body with happiness and her boldness to see what there was in the world. Her name was Rose, but she loved sunflowers, they were her favorite. I remember her tattoo of sunflowers spread across her shoulder adding to every perfectly placed feature she had. She cared about people, but others had broken her and let her down before. She always tried to lighten up the days of others because she knew how painful this world could be.

She hesitated to answer my question before revealing a bright smile and asking, "Oh, it's a date?" I softly responded, "Why not? It wasn't going to be but I'm asking you now. Is that okay with you Rose?" her green eyes were the only thing preventing my heart from beating out of control or possibly out of my chest. "Yes, that's... That sounds good!" she said without breaking her seamlessly perfect smile. "Good it will be fun, you have my word," I told her with pure confidence.

As Friday appeared I was wary, but more so excited because I was comfortable with her next to me. We met at the restaurant and I told her we were going ice skating at the Crown Center in Kansas City. It was a popular shopping center that flowed with people, a place where the air was brimming with happiness. Once we arrived we made our way into the shopping center to explore. We shared stories of other trips to the city and our childhood which led us into the Crayola crayon store. We wrote our names on the paper board just before leaving for the toy store. I asked her questions because every answer I received made me even more curious about her.

We walked around in search of a good place to eat before deciding on a popular burger restaurant. Once we were swollen from excessive amounts of food, we decided to head for the ice rink. Truthfully I was not prepared, I was never bad but also not good at any form of skating. So as we stopped to look at an indoor waterfall I found a perfect tool I could use to stall. I took a seat and corrected my posture before asking her to be kind in her judgment. I began to play the piano, chord by chord through what poor memory I have. I played some classics before playing an original I had just thought up, inspired by her presence.

She sat next to me and I showed her chords that sound perfect together. She took a picture of me without me realizing and I looked at her just quick enough to see her blush turn into a smile, a beautiful smile. As she sat next to me I could feel her watching me and I could smell the cold weather and the sweet vanilla radiating from her body. In that moment I found what was missing, what had been taken from me previously. This girl had not taken it, but she could offer it to me, which made me grateful. She could offer me happiness, security, and warmth again. In return, I would keep her just as warm, happy, and safe as I longed to be.

Once we had found our way to the ice rink I was even worse than I remembered and quickly befriended the floor. But Rose... she was stunning as she glided across the ice only making mistakes for my satisfaction. The ice was no longer cold as she leaned against me to take a picture of us together. Just as the camera had, my eyes captured her smile at that very moment. That photo lived in my head constantly as we drove back to her car that night. I thought about kissing her, but I worried it was too soon. Before departing I asked her to text me when she was home so I would be assured she was alright, so she did.

I arrived at work the next day slightly before Rose and was instantly assailed with questions about how the date had gone. I did my best not to show my emotions, as I had been so recently accustomed to hiding them, which only worried my co-workers. But I assured them I had a great time and that she had enthralled my thoughts the entirety of the night. That held them off until Rose's friend walked through the open doorway. She demanded a walk-through of the night, and I obliged because it had been coursing through my thoughts all morning anyway.

Not long after I finished the story, Rose appeared from the other side of the restaurant. Her hair loose in a messy bun and makeup slept on from the previous night, she was just as beautiful if not more. I walked to the small windowless room in which we took our breaks to intersect her. "Hi" I began, revealing only part of my smile. "Hiii" she grinned while turning to look into my eyes. My thoughts instantly demanded that it be the last "Hi" we ever shared. There was simply no need for "Hi" if we never said goodbye to each other.

During our shift together the air was dense with words not spoken but implied to each other. It is as if the magic that had flown through the air the previous night had flooded over into that day. We talked lightly and agreed to talk further after we both got off of work. As she grabbed her coat and prepared herself to leave, I stood and marveled at her every movement before walking her out. We reached her car and we both got in to plan our next date for the following evening. After spending time in the car and after many prolonged hugs I remembered something a co-worker had told me.

"So someone mentioned you were wondering as to why I did not kiss you last night?" She chuckled, "Wow no, I was just talking about it, I don't mind. But why didn't you?" she replied. I took her hand and waited a few seconds "I wanted you to be comfortable and respected," I stated.

Then I inched closer and softened my voice to match the subtle song that played through the car. I continued "But yesterday was our first date, and tomorrow is our second so... I am going to kiss you now." Just before my lips could close from sounding the "w", they touched hers and fell in sync with how hers moved. Minutes continued passing and we had only moved closer to absorb the heat radiating off each other.

We faded from each other's firm grasps and leaned into the same positions that we were in moments before. I stared into her eyes only to be greeted with green emeralds that sparkled as if they belonged among the stars. Not long passed before she demanded I break my gaze while giggling and shoving my arm from the console. Unlike other relationships I had been in, she did not enjoy it when I stared at her. I only ever stared immensely at a woman if I was truly perplexed by their beauty. Quickly, I began to realize this was way more than a crush and I would never have enough of her.

It seemed like Ella had escaped my mind, but she was only really buried beneath what I felt for Rose. As I laid in bed that night, every moment since Ella and I met played across the black ceiling. I was projecting these moments in my head across a blank, dark surface because they had been trapped in my mind for far too long. I finally began to find hidden memories of Ella that meant something more to me than the rest. I immediately demanded my body to sleep and shoved every suffocating memory down as far as possible. The memory that changed that night for me was when Ella had first taken me to one of our favorite picnic spots. It was near a lake and I could hear her giggle as she took my hand and dragged me near the water. It was happy...

I instantly blocked that image and closed my mind to any more memories, to think only of my future. I would not let my past interrupt my future with Rose. After hours of constant and vigorous tossing around in my bed, I had finally fallen asleep. The next morning I went to school and once 8th period had come, I was excited to share my weekend tale with Angelina. She was very happy for me and my newfound relationship with Rose.

Angelina was always there to listen to me and tell me how stupid or fortunate I was. No matter what kind of day she was having, she always listened. She was always a great supporter and very brave given everything she had been through with her own life. She never let onto the struggles that weighed her down, but you could hear her body aching under the pressure. She was always worried about family and friends instead of herself. She was young, yet so full of passion and excitement. At times she would need a break and I would be there for her, I was thankful she was there for me.

In the following weeks, Rose and I started to become slightly frustrated because it was difficult to find time for each other. We had gone throughout the week only seeing each other at work. That Friday, which was my birthday, my family was doing some sort of small party and I invited her along not knowing the arrangements my family had made.

I picked her up from work and met my parents at a pizza restaurant nearby. We had reserved a table and once my family arrived they explained that we were going axe throwing a few doors down. It was fun, and Rose interacted with my niece and nephew so well. It was truly one of my favorite birthdays. We eventually left and I went to drop her off back at her car. We talked for a while and once I began to kiss her goodnight she began to press the gas on the running car. I laughed hysterically as her cheeks glowed red from embarrassment. It was always the simple things that she did that had left me grinning in satisfaction.

After that night we still struggled to find time for each other. When we did, some of the time we would waste arguing a little. It was never bad and it was always over something simple. I was and have always been jealous and protective over my relationships because they are of so much value to me. I would put all my effort into the relationships and they became my life, of course I would be jealous. I told her we needed to get away and just enjoy the company of each other. "Let's go to St. Louis. It's not a big vacation but we could get away

proposed. She giggled and responded, "Okay, I'm down. When are we going to go though?" Caught off guard by her response I grinned, "Oh um, January, why not?"

A couple of weeks had passed since my suggestion and we were finally buying train tickets for our three-day weekend away. It was exciting and nerve-racking all at once. We saw the order confirmations ring in as we kissed and continued on our date of playing pool and arcade games. We had both mentioned this trip to our parents. At the time, my parents thought nothing of it. The following day I told my parents we had bought the tickets and were for sure going. They were shocked and somewhat upset because I had obligations those days, but I knew I needed to do this.

I had found a way around my obligations and even made reservations for a restaurant in St. Louis. For Christmas, one of her gifts was the surprise reservation. The restaurant was on top of a hotel with a direct view of the gateway arch and the city's illustrious skyline. Thoughts of the trip left us happy and excited.

It was finally the morning of the trip and I spent the majority of the night awake in excitement and anticipation. Rose and her mother had agreed to come out of their way to pick me up so I did not have to leave my car anywhere. It was approximately 5 a.m. when we left my house and an hour later we arrived at the train station. After exploring the station and sitting on a bench with her head against mine for another hour we boarded the train. The entire ride was about 5 hours of listening to music and sleeping. As we grew closer to the city, Rose discovered she had big projects that were due by the end of the night for two of her college credit classes. She began to stress and apologize because she would have to do them once we arrived. I simply reassured her and pulled her close to comfort her in the warmth of my arms. Refraining from allowing my icy, frigid hands to touch her bare skin.

Once we arrived, we Ubered to the luxury apartment we had rented for the next two days. We were dropped off at the wrong location, but we did not mind walking and seeing the city on our way to our accommodations. Once we obtained the keys, I unlocked the door and held it as Rose entered the space with a gasp. Without proper time to even take in the beauty of the apartment or city, we unpacked. She said she would go to the library across the street to do her homework alone, but I insisted on staying with her.

We arrived at the library and after she had gone to the computer and logged in, I kissed her head and sat in a reading chair 20 feet away. She hated when I stared at her so I did my best to stay occupied, but I continuously caught myself staring in awe in her direction. I had fallen asleep, but upon waking I asked how she was progressing. She then indicated she still had much to do. I told her I was going to the apartment to grab something and I would return to her shortly.

I was really only going to a coffee shop nearby to surprise her, but I was also in need of fresh air. I grabbed a coffee for myself and a vanilla latte for her, her favorite. She was grateful for her surprise and sincerely apologetic for me having to wait for her to finish the assignments. I wished she didn't have to, but I was grateful to be there with her, away from the other obligations that bound us at home. It was late now and the library was closing, so we had gone back to our apartment where she continued her homework on her phone. I showered and poured us each a glass of wine as she asked herself questions aloud about English and History. I responded and she looked at me in shock that I knew such particular facts. She began to say the questions more quietly thinking I would not hear her. I would then come close to her and quietly whisper the answer in her ear. It didn't take long for her to hook a pillow directly into my jaw before mumbling a thank you.

Once she finished her homework I helped her up and helped her ready herself for the evening ahead. I would pull outfits from her suitcase awaiting her approval. After many ill-approved outfits, I tossed a white sweater in her direction. That night we went to a restaurant directly under our apartment. We were the only ones there and I couldn't help but remark about my infatuation for her. She scanned the room for a distraction so she would not have to look me in the eyes when I told her how beautiful she was. Once I saw this, I reached my hand across the table and pulled her chin to face me as I told her to look at me. She then grinned as her eyes began to widen and her breathing slowed. We both knew it was time for us to leave before the tension swallowed the room.

Back at the apartment, we were playing some music and talked. Every sentence drew our bodies closer and our eyes to each other's lips. I looked once more into her eyes before pulling her in and kissing her. The kisses then began to repeat time and time again before I pulled away and looked at her. "I know we decided this word was tossed around too lightly in relationships and we agreed to wait, but I would be lying if I told you I haven't been in love with you for a while now." There was a moment of hesitation before she kissed me and backed away to respond, "I love you". My eyes widened as I tackled her to the couch and kissed her repeatedly, moving from her lips to her neck. We looked at each other and it was pure happiness coursing through our veins.

We slept on the living room floor that night with only blankets. The next morning we woke up early to explore the city. We found ourselves at a cozy spot for brunch nearby. We then went to buy groceries which we brought to the apartment and cleaned up before heading to the city's tourist hotspot, Union Station. We went to the aquarium and looked through the gift shop. We then went to the botanical garden where we marveled together at the alluring landscape.

It was cold once we left and we went back to the apartment to prepare for our much-anticipated dinner reservation. Once we arrived we were escorted to the top floor where we chose our table. The food was delicious but the view was spectacular. I wish I could have enjoyed the view more but in comparison to Rose, it was tragically less marvelous. I was fortunate enough to experience it with her, experience the entire getaway with her.

Once we returned to the apartment building I took her to our second highlight destination of the evening. I guided her out as she looked in confusion, which quickly changed into marvel at yet another beautiful view. I then pulled her to the nearby door parallel from us and swiped the key card. After a sudden click, we opened the door to a two-story lounge. We racked a game of billiards, then went to the balcony where we were able to see the St. Louis Arch again, this time in private. After returning to the apartment we listened to music and held each other till the sun rose the next day.

After a few hours, she was not up yet and I was unable to go back to sleep, so I prepared some coffee. I then began eggs and toast that I quickly plated and took to the bedroom. I kissed her head and whispered her name as she waved me away, but quickly came around after she smelled breakfast. Once we ate, we showered and when she emerged into the bedroom wearing only a towel I was compelled by her beauty. I told her to look at me as I began to stare and I grabbed her to pull her onto my lap. Her eyes screaming of insecurity and begging for comfort pulled me into her lips. I quickly pulled her next to me on the bed and began kissing her neck. Just as she grabbed my hair I grabbed her hand and pushed it into the pillow. I ripped the towel off and pulled her up just as the phone rang.

At once we both looked at the phone then at each other in panic and rushed to get dressed. We both knew it was the renter so we raced to pack our things as we were late to check out. Once we had made it onto the train there was a feeling that lingered. We began to speak of when we would see each other next once we were home, which quickly turned to frustration. We had not even arrived at home yet, but it felt like we were already apart from one another.

We didn't have time to speak for a while after St. Louis and I began dreading an upcoming trip she was going on. Before we began dating she bought tickets with a male friend of hers to visit her sister in Australia. She could tell me not to worry but I had heard that before from other voices, and that only caused more frustration. I wanted to trust her, I did, but we were just getting started and I did not want to jeopardize that.

Just slightly over a week had passed and she was on a plane with a man I had not met, headed to another country. I was hopefully optimistic and felt as though I must trust her. Given my past, I could not shake the fear of something happening that would cause our split. Instead, I attempted to be happy for her getting to see the world and hid my true feelings. I couldn't help but feel I should be the one with her, that I should experience every part this world has to offer with her.

There had only been a few arguments over Facetime while she was away. One of them had been because she mentioned staying an extra few days in Hawaii on their layover from Australia. She told me her sister bought the new tickets without her knowledge. Of course, I needed to let her enjoy the trip but I was upset I had to wait longer for her return.

My frustration subsided while she stayed the additional days in Hawaii and returned after nearly a month away. This had pulled on our relationship, but I was just happy to have her by my side once again. A day later we made plans to have dinner with her family, so we met prior at work and rode together. The dinner was fun and enjoyable until her sister had mentioned coming back days ago. I was quickly confused. My mood changed drastically and I had to perform the smile that I had faked so often before. I came to attention once again as I heard Rose repeat my name and insist I tell her what was wrong. I told her nothing and set aside my feelings for later.

The drive to her car was quiet and I didn't dare bring up her lies because she was resting her head on my arm and I feared not having that anymore. I got home and slept to the thoughts of what could have actually happened in Hawaii. Was she even in Hawaii for longer than they expected or was that simply a lie so that she would not have to see me?

A few days had passed and my true emotions were silenced, conversation became tasteless and trite. It was late on a cool Monday night when she called me and demanded I meet her halfway between our houses. I asked her if it was something we were able to discuss at another time because I had work to finish. Just as before, something had altered between us and I was worried. I had seen this happen before and I knew what needed to happen but I did not have the strength to face it. She insisted we meet, and that night she told me we were breaking up. She admitted lying to me about where she had been and who she was with. My heart pulsed slowly and heavily as all other sounds but her voice faded. That was supposed to be the last of it, I knew I should have gotten into my car and driven away, but I didn't. I quieted my emotions that were brimming with anguish and ire. I looked at her once again and wiped a falling tear from her sorrowful face. I asked her if she was sorry and if she would do it again. "No, I wouldn't and I'm so sorry!" she whimpered. After a moment I sighed, "Okay, then we're not breaking up, just don't ever do that again or take me for granted. I don't want to be without you so just promise me to try to work on it?"

We made up and parted ways that night, heading in two different directions. A piece of us broke that night and a piece of my pain from Ella resurfaced to remind me what was coming. I do not blame Rose, I can be controlling. I exercise control because I've lost so much in my life already. I have become better with my tendencies, but the feeling of control in a world where I am so controlless is intoxicating. I was addicted to that intoxication, it would either destroy my thoughts and happiness or destroy my relationship. However, I knew of my faults and did all that I was able to cover them with gestures that make relationships seemingly perfect. The world would be in our hands just as long as my partners looked past my traumatic faults.

We saw each other after that, not very often because of our busy schedules, but just enough to be considered in a relationship. Valentine's Day was creeping in and I was determined to rekindle what magic was once between us. We had plans to hang out that evening and exchange gifts. As it grew closer we both were getting more excited to celebrate what we had.

Once we met, I drove her to the location of our first date. Just as before, we explored the shops and went through a catwalk that had a beautiful view of the city. A few weeks back Ella had texted me and I responded. Ella and I had a typical conversation inquiring of each other's well-being, that was all. Rose and I were going to take a picture together with the city behind us. She opened up my phone and as she navigated to the camera she passed by Ella's messages. Her expression changed as she deflated and settled on an emotionless face. I apologized for not telling her and quickly explained that it was just a normal conversation. I told her to look through the messages to verify and she began to, then stopped and handed me the phone.

She told me she wanted to go home and I begged her to look and understand the messages were typical and banal. She insisted we leave, and the silence was suffocating. By the time we reached my car, my cheeks had been red from withholding the silent tears that expected to escape. Once we were back at her car we exchanged Valentine's gifts, but with the same tone she had the past hour, she voiced she was going home. The night was early and I pleaded for her to stay, assuring her that she was the only one that meant a thing to me. I'm not sure that was true, but I know I never would have intentionally hurt her. After many shed tears, she complied and we went to get ice cream. The cold ice cream melted on our tongues and resulted in a slight smile, but it truly changed nothing. We went home that night both knowing that we argued more than we should over what little time we had together.

A few days later we had planned to hang out but she had made other plans without me. I was immensely frustrated with our lack of time together so she told me to go home and I did just that.

Before I could make it home she called me and told me she wanted to break up and despite my defiance she was persistent. I pleaded once more "Rose let's talk about this, just meet me and we can figure this out."

Chapter 10

Spotify Chapter 10 Playlist

https://open.spotify.com/playlist/25kbKrUA39wAaTVeUK8JRF

Amazon Chapter 10 Playlist

https://music.amazon.com/user-playlists/4a2c9ace84dc405aa597e35a8566ac
dcsune?marketplaceId=ATVPDKIKX0DER&musicTerritory=US

Chapter 10
Desmond's Despair

We only met once after that night and it was simply to return the other's possessions. Once again I was alone and left with only my thoughts to shred what little happiness that remained. The breakup not only left me alone with my feelings for Rose but also reemerged the pain that Ella left. I crave to know how they felt when they both left me, was it easy?

How do I relieve this pain that pulses through my body constantly aching to be felt? The same pain that revolts at the sight of Ella and Rose. It does not revolt because it hates them for what they did, but it revolts at the sight of them because it misses them. I loved Rose but a few months were truly no match for the happiness I was stripped of when Ella left me. Ella's warm hazel eyes now appear in every face I see and her figure appeared in every place I found myself for the next few months. I expected it to get easier after a week but the pain never subsided and my thoughts continued to punish me for what mistakes I may have made. She once told our friends that she was thankful for me, but then I realized she wasn't. She was thankful for the attention and care I gave her. Just the other day I could smell her same perfume and see those same soft hazel eyes.

I kept wanting her to tell me what was so terrible about me that she had to leave me. What is so much better about him? Ella's beauty towered over every girl I saw from then on. Every girl became so tasteless when compared to her. She was a drug and I was addicted, but when I was stripped from that I had to find a new drug to further my high. Rose was that drug and it worked well, but that drug was now gone too. I was desperate and every emotion that had been pushed aside by the high was resurfacing, bringing endless sadness with it.

Every time I am forced to pass by the community center, I still look for Ella's truck. Some people have told me there will always be hard times that come with the good, and this was hard. I'm suffering to atone for the happiness I had with them. Ella was so much more to me than a relationship, she became a part of my life and every day without her and without Rose was gut-wrenching. The memories of Ella and I together should be slipping from my mind by now but instead, they are playing on repeat to consume my monotonous days.

I know that she doesn't care at all, not anymore. I could see both relationships begin to fail, but I was so concerned with the ending that I failed to recognize the signs. I was now searching for any real device to subdue the misery I was in. Nothing had prepared me for what the pain of losing love would feel like. The pain was immensely excruciating, even compared to the pain of my heart racing at 200 bpm.

Without love I had so little, I had given up so much to solely focus on being the best bachelor I could be and it led me to pain only comparable to losing a piece of myself. It was a privilege to be loved by Ella and I was so concerned with the small things like what I was having for dinner, that I didn't appreciate the warmth of her soft skin. She wasn't my girlfriend, she was my princess, she was my friend... my best friend. Her accomplishments were so great and I should have told her how proud I was of her for who she became. She was so smart and was a diligent worker. Rose was beautiful and fun and she made the pain disappear, but Ella made me a better person, someone I was proud to be. Now I can only be disappointed in myself for letting go of Ella.

When I hear Ella's name, my muscles weaken and my mind numbs with pain. After a moment the rest of my body fills with the same numbness and paralyzes me where I stand. When Ella and I first began to talk this happened to me, but the only difference was that now my smile was weighed down by the pain of losing her. How do I rid my mind of her when she became all I thought of for two years? The vices worked but only temporarily, Rose also worked but when she left it forced me to think I was the problem.

My friends and family were not oblivious to my sadness but didn't know how to help me. "I'm fine" became the phrase that I spoke the most. "I'm so lost" became the phrase I most commonly thought. I wanted to silence my thoughts, maybe then I would be able to have peace, or be content. I hoped that silence in my head would allow me to sleep and that sleep would allow me to be happy again. I knew I would be happy once again, but I wanted to be happy now.

Truthfully I knew that I would never find someone like Ella, and at the time that scared me. I think that one of the things that made our breakup so difficult is because I was left to my thoughts. After Rose and Ella left, my mind turned against me. I want to say that I kept up with the world but even then my heart was still spread across the parking lot the night Ella told me to go home. In the year since that day, the whole world continued to move while I was stuck in that same damn parking lot. My heart was still bruised and bleeding from the pain she caused. She found someone new while I reminisced about what was because I am too afraid to face that she no longer thinks of me. I was silly to consider myself the plot of her book, I was merely a chapter. But she was the main character in mine.

Just as I opened my eyes it was three weeks later on a Monday. My thoughts had consumed me, so I went to the park behind the hotel that Ella and

I frequently went to. I walked through the park with her ghost, telling her about the past few weeks and as I reached one end of the park, the ghost of Rose appeared on my other side. I told Rose that she gave me hope in finding love again and that I wouldn't trade our recent trip to St. Louis for anything. After I said this her ghost vanished, and once again it was just Ella and me. We reached the entrance to the park again and I paused to look at her apparition. I wanted to ask her why she was here. I knew it was only because I allowed her to be. So instead, "why did you leave me?" is what I blurted to the spring air next to me. I heard no response and began to yell, "Why won't you answer me? Two years and then you realized there was something so wrong with me! Just leave then because I have changed and I know I made mistakes, but I also gave you everything I had!" She then disappeared from my sight, but not from my mind.

I began to scroll through pictures over and over again searching through every date we had been on. I looked at how happy I was when I was in the presence of her smile. Both Rose and Ella were beautiful, but I never knew Rose as I did Ella. Ella struggled and yet still managed to care about people around her, she wanted to be a doctor. I loved the way she talked about medicine so much that for a while it made me want to go into the field. There was a level of joy in her voice when she talked about her passions that was contagious. But since that night I have simply had to watch her dissolve into the love and affection of another man. My heart, which was now numb, merely pumped less for the things I was once passionate about.

Without love, my life had grown monotonous and bland. Days were repetitive and the only thing in my life that seemed stable were my thoughts about the amazing women I had driven away. I simply had nothing without a girlfriend because so much of my recent time was spent as a boyfriend. I focused solely on being the best I could be for my future wife, but it felt like my future wife had already left me. The times we argued about where she was and who she was with pulsed through my head, reminding me why she was right to leave me. The walls that surrounded my heart had been knocked down twice now and I had no idea how to repair them.

Ella told me she saw the word "love" as serious and when she said it, she meant it. She told me she loved me often, but now she is saying it to another man. I may be bitter or shattered by her actions, but I was serious when I told her I loved her. I want to stop seeing Ella's ghost. I want to stop waiting for a notification to appear with Ella's name. I want her to be proud of who I am... I want to be happy again!

I still play the song that I had written the night Rose and I first went out. I play it repeatedly to remind myself that I have let go of something that relieved the pain that this world had placed on me. At times I can't finish it because it's Ella's phantom that appears and plays next to me. Just like we used to do after her practice with her theater group. They would watch us perform a duet together, reciting every word and playing every chord from memory. It's a good memory but then I snap out of it as the piano bench slips from under me to lay me on the floor. I would sit on the floor allowing my thoughts to deprive me of the energy to get up and be productive.

I became sick at the thought of food. I laid in my bed at night dreading the next day because then I would have to fake a smile for the rest of the world. I was accustomed to fake smiles by that point but still found myself staring into the distance awaiting the ghost of Ella. It became a common occurrence and I felt my mind slipping from reality because my reality was no longer a place I wanted to live. At least in my mind, she was there. In my head, I could be whoever I wanted and love whoever I wanted. The best part was that in my mind, she couldn't just walk away from me as they both did. It was painful to think of Ella in the real world. But when she lived in the universe of my mind, it was numb just like the rest of my body.

I was simply a fool to think Ella's love was forever, it was a completely unachievable promise to hold. I was inevitably bound to fall for her. Not because of her body or her perfect smile, but because of her personality, her energy, and her every self-proclaimed flaw. Truthfully she didn't have flaws, they were only beautiful scars. I understood that pain and I understood how beautiful it was that she survived the pain that left her with those beautiful scars.

Over a month had passed since Rose left me and every day was a blur of emotion. The voices in my head echoed the memories of all the dates I had been on. Everything had been so colorful when I was with Ella or Rose, but now the world appeared so dull and grey. I was now stripped of happiness, letting the world pass me by until I could watch the colors of the world bloom again. I knew I would see

Ella again, but what would I say to a face that caused so much pain, so much despair.

Ella told me she would be my princess for the rest of my life. The problem is that she is now the queen to someone else. It hurts horrifically to think of Ella with another man. My gut wrenches, my heart palpitates rapidly, and my mind aches at the sight of her in the arms of another. I was sure she was not being treated as well as I would treat her, but maybe that's the point. Even though the pain pulses through my body at the sight of her with her new boyfriend, she looks happy. We also looked happy together, but that means nothing of what happens when no one is watching. It hurts, but if I look past all of the sadness there is a piece of me that is happy for who she is now. That is how I know I loved her.

Ella's phantom had been dancing through my head and showed its face once more. The anguish and frustration that I had submerged deep beneath my pulsing heart had reappeared. The world still passed me by in a blur, but I finally began to move. It was as though my body was taking me somewhere. I first passed by her work, then to an abandoned parking lot where my shivering hand placed the car in park. Her phantom was in my passenger seat staring at me in anticipation. The world around my car began to spin, gaining speed every moment. Then my lips which had been sealed by the fake smile opened and I bellowed...

"I dreamt of you a few nights ago, did you think of me? They say that some people have a connection so that when the first person thinks of the second, the second person then also thinks of the first. It is crazy because it has been a year since we broke up and I am sitting here thinking that my life will never be the same. I know my life will never be the same. Honestly, I am stuck in a position I've never experienced before and I have no clue how to get out. I have been thinking about you often, but if I could go back I would not change anything. I'm different than I was then, and I know you are too. Even if you never wanted me to change when you left me, I did because I could not bear to see the same person in the mirror that you left.

You have built something inside of me that has numbed me to certain emotions that most people feel. I was the sweet boy that did no harm and saw making love as special. But when I make love to any woman now, I just want to punish her for the mistakes you made, the mistakes I made. You have taught me that I truly have no control over who or what breaks me. So now when I screw someone, I take control of them because it is the only time I am able to feel in control. I tie her to the frame of the silk draped bed because she won't run from me just as you did. I trace a map of her body with my lips because I still remember the location of your every freckle. I tease her because you teased me time and time again before you left me. NOW I WILL NEVER LOOK AT THE LAKE WE USED TO GO TO WITHOUT SEEING YOUR GHOST!

You haunt me and I hear your voice say my name constantly while I stare into the distance waiting for you to appear. But you do not, you are never there because you have moved on and I have just moved. Your ghost still haunts me but I am numb to it, I don't love you Ella, but I crave your presence. I just have to know if you think of me when you go to that lake too? Do you think of the time we ran through the sprinklers on the museum lawn? Or even when you see the sushi restaurant we would always go to, am I there waiting? Does my name or the music I play still ring through your head? It is not that you are no longer worth my time, it's that you occupied so much of my time that my mind is confused as to why you are now gone. I have changed and I am beyond grateful for who I have become, are you? Please tell me, when he looks at you, do you ever see me looking back?"

My head instantly dropped as I gasped to regain the breath I had lost. Everything had stopped spinning and I pulled my head up, which was still heavy from exhaustion and looked to my passenger seat. She looked at me with a smile as tears poured from her warm hazel brown eyes. It was a sight I had been without for so long and it had not lost a fragment of beauty, but it hurt to see her like this. I wiped my still running nose and sighed "hey, it's okay". Her smile grew and just as I reached to wipe the tears from her perfect rosy cheeks, she vanished.

Chapter 11

Spotify Chapter 11 Playlist

https://open.spotify.com/playlist/28eIk7ncFyJNpD40afcBpB

Amazon Chapter 11 Playlist

https://music.amazon.com/user-playlists/3dc1967e94714f2d99136ef8495577
e7sune?marketplaceId=ATVPDKIKX0DER&musicTerritory=US

Chapter 11
Euphoria

That was the last time I saw Ella, or at least her phantom that corrupted my mind. I was stripped from the most powerful drug I have ever used, it is understandable to have withdrawal. The following day after the ghost of Ella vanished, I woke up in sync with the world that surrounded me. Ella still crossed my mind throughout the day, but it was numb. There was no pain as if I had been released from the chains she had bound me with. I was happy, but only because of my newfound feeling of freedom and peace.

The next day was similar in my feeling of peace, but I was also once again able to think of more than just the pain that my exes bestowed upon me. I thought of my promise to become the knight in shining armor which I saw in all of the films. I was once again determined to become that man that every girl sought to find. I have changed since my freshman year and gained a lot of useful knowledge that will assist me with this resolution. I appeared in the mirror and looked up to see myself once again. "You lost them, but you will not lose the next" I asserted to the confident figure I saw in the mirror. This was the beginning of what I first set out to do, and I was determined to accomplish this goal.

The next morning was the beginning of April and I began a routine where I started with breakfast and online work. I then took a shower and ate lunch before preparing for work. Once I came home I would work out and prepare for bed only to repeat the next day. As monotonous as it seems, I changed the routine regularly to prevent banality. I also began to practice and refine my ability to play the piano. I was able to see myself changing as I worked to be a better form of myself. The passion had returned to my eyes and others began to notice as they saw who I was becoming.

My wardrobe changed as well. I dressed proper and intellectual before, but then I started wearing refined and sensual clothing. Wal-Mart cologne had changed into Dior and Versace. I was a man turning myself into a gentleman. I was something I appreciated, but I then molded myself into something to be desired. I had no intention of changing my personality, that had evolved itself. But a personality is less useful without the attraction of other people.

I had been so lost in the pain that there was no room for appreciation of myself. I hid my wounds and pain from the world because they were still sore, still bleeding. Now those wounds have turned into scars, scars that I wear openly in hopes others see them. There is a beauty in my scars just as there was a beauty in Ella's. This has not depleted my appreciation of Ella but rather increased my appreciation for myself. I realized that nothing will change the pain she caused me, but I can change the pain that I cause myself. I focused so much on being there for others that I had no time left for myself.

It was only weeks ago that I sat in sorrow over the sadness life had placed on me. Now I simply aspire for the day my future wife wakes next to me in a bed of silk under the light from a sunrise beaming through the Emerald City known as Seattle. Ever since Ella, I have been fascinated with the sensation of power, the possibility of success. It was not about the world making me dreary, it was merely that I focused on one source of happiness that had left me. This world is full of happiness and potential, it surrounds us. I was clueless of life and oblivious of love when all I had to do was open my eyes to the possibilities. That day in the parking lot when I was with Ella's ghost, I released all of the frustration that had simmered in my body. I then filled that empty space with passion, not for her but for my future.

"For so long I held you close because refraining from chasing you would be the most difficult thing I could do. It was one of the most difficult things I have ever done, but I realized it was time to let go, let you go" I remarked. I craved the love of another woman but knew that I was not prepared for that. A relationship at this time would distract me from my goals and my future. I am not able to be who I want to become without first appreciating myself. I must appreciate who I am before I grow an appreciation for anyone else.

Until recently, looking back on the breakups only brought pain and sadness. Now aside from the pain, when I looked back at the breakups, they reminded me it was an opportunity. An opportunity to regain the confidence I had lost, an opportunity to become my own idol. This was a singular road that I realized I had to walk in order to accept myself. I did not want to rid my mind of Ella and Rose, but rather I wanted to appreciate what I had aside from them. I was so focused on the idea of them and their beauty that I hadn't noticed the beauty in the world that surrounded me. The comfort they gave me was irreplaceable, but the love that I found for myself and my family was even more drastic. They were only winning the war that waged in my mind because I had let them.

For so long after the breakups, I was desperate to feel the same love I had with them. However, there is no one like them and I should not seek someone who has no interest in me. My standards were raised and I became well aware of what I truly deserved. I was becoming emotionally independent and free. Ella had ripped me of my love for eye contact, but I was no longer bound by her restraints. I had regained my love for eye contact and the emotions that could be conveyed in eye contact. My eyes were always an attraction for others because of their cold blue-grey color. There was no longer a battle among my thoughts, it was over and I had won.

I did not only become emotionally free, but I was also financially free. I had always desired to treat Ella and Rose with the finest memories. Unfortunately, the best memories were not always cheap. I had established a written financial plan for myself that included expenses, savings, travel money, and investments. It was now around the spring of 2020 and the stock market had fallen due to the Covid-19 virus. The world was falling into chaos and I saw this as an opportunity to invest in the stock market. I was financially stable and there were no dates to pay for. I only paid for myself and what I wanted. I was stable enough that I could afford to donate to the homeless and less fortunate. I would buy dessert at restaurants and set money aside to donate to different charities. I could not do this often but was happy to help when I could.

During my transformation, I was not only focused on becoming who I wanted to be but I was also learning who it was that I truly wanted to be. I no longer stayed up all night thinking of what could be, but I did stay up. Now thinking of new ways to better myself and better my career. I thought of how Ella, Rose, and the rest of my friends would see me once I became like the people that once intimidated me.

I still visited some of the parks that Ella and I would go to, but I never saw her ghost, nor did I want to. I would simply sit in the park with a coffee and read. This was not to bask in my recent freedom from her, but rather to bask in the beauty. The same beauty the world had to offer when we were together, only I no longer needed her to see the beauty. Though I no longer needed her, I was by no means deserting her. If she needed my help today, I would still assist her. She was a big part of my life and that will forever matter to me.

I have met other spectacular and beautiful women since Rose. However, there was never a spark like there was with Ella. So they were simply not a priority, and I knew I would be a fool to involve them if they were not a priority to me. Truthfully, my definition of spark had changed since I was with Ella. What Ella and I had was sincere and magical but not a spark or a flame. I had finally realized the spark was not when I caught her fall while drowning in her glossy hazel eyes. No, the spark was when Ella left me because I then knew that I had to become who I wanted and not who she wanted me to be. The flame was not our love, the flame was the change that had been occurring ever since the night my feet trudged across the parking lot where she left me.

The year 2020 had resulted in many people changing drastically. It was full of isolation, loneliness, responsibility, and chaos. There was little feeling of safety because the illness that ravaged the world was invisible. It was near impossible to avoid something that was not visible to the human eye. Jobs were constantly at stake and schooling was dramatically impaired. Truthfully, it was a cheerless year that forced every young adult into maturity.

Though I was free from the pain she had placed upon me, my life was far from simple. Not every day was euphoric and happy. Some days Ella still crossed my mind with a shred of pain left behind from another time. She was my forever and I have not felt the same way again. I was over her, but the idea of her still settled in the abyss of my mind. I was happy where I was even if she was no longer a part of my life. I was truly happy with who

I was becoming and I would not jeopardize that. I learned to be patient with myself and with the possibility of love. Honestly, I would have learned nothing that I know now if it wasn't for her. I finally forgave her, I forgave myself.

Chapter 12

Spotify Chapter 12 Playlist

https://open.spotify.com/playlist/4ZAF3xwq5bs9hlJ4qyz51W

Amazon Chapter 12 Playlist

https://music.amazon.com/user-playlists/f39e6df1b4a94779bff72651fb958f9
dsune?marketplaceId=ATVPDKIKX0DER&musicTerritory=US

Chapter 12
Bona Fide

The memories of this time began to drift away as my head began to ache with pain. My brain pulsed and the world around me began to fade into a kaleidoscope of colors. I began to fear I was having another bad episode as I fell to my knees. I was then only light-headed while I trembled to find my feet. After a moment of disorientation, I stood once again. I heard a voice speak, a voice that wasn't mine. It was the same voice that sounded through my mind the night my heart betrayed me. "If the people of your past were standing in front of you right now, what would you say to them?" the voice echoed through my throbbing head.

I was staggered by the question, but I was compelled to answer. Emotions once again raced through my numb body to fill what was seemingly lifeless. After pondering a diligent answer I hid my feeling of shock behind a half-smirk. They appeared in front of me with my memories flashing rapidly. At last, I was energized with the words to express what I would say to the people of my past.

"Dear Rose, I hope you are well and just as happy as I knew you to be. I still remember the joy when we agreed to go on a date together. At times I know that you wondered if you meant very much to me, but you did. Though we were not together for very long, you helped me to become the man that I am today and I am grateful. I am grateful for the happiness you gave me when we were together. I will forever remember our trip to St. Louis and think fondly upon it.

You were so very beautiful in many ways. You were kind-hearted, carefree, and always willing to challenge the life in front of us. That added greatly to your beauty and to the attraction that pulled me into your life. I consider you to be a friend and girlfriend that has motivated me to be better. I always worked to make you happy and I hope that you realize that, as well as understand I had no intention to ever jeopardize your happiness. Sadly, there was an increasing amount of arguments between us that were not necessary. I blinded myself from the arguments and focused on our happiness because I feared what followed. I was not yet ready to be alone again, I was not ready to lose someone who I had grown so infatuated with.

Aside from your extravagant beauty, you were smart. I hope that the people who are blessed to be in your life in the future are kind to you. You are intelligent enough to find the best for yourself. I believe that because you were smart enough to see that we weren't meant for each other, even if I was blinded by it at the time. I hope to see you again, I hope to see you just as happy and blissful as you deserve.

One of my happiest moments was when we ate sherbert in bed late one night when we had both fallen ill."

"As for my friends and enemies, thank you.

Without my enemies who treated me with disrespect, I would not be who I am now. So those of you who were cruel, I wish for you to be better, but I hope you are satisfied with my changes. I understand you wanted to see my failure, but you only made me stronger.

My friends, I am grateful for the important roles that you played in my life. I am glad you challenged me to become better and gave me unforgettable memories."

"I am beyond grateful for the sacrifices my parents and family have made for me. I was not easy to deal with at times, but I am thankful for the environment I was given to grow into. I hope you are proud of who I have become, and I hope to show my gratitude for years to come. I likely would not have made it to where I am today without all of you to help me through my hardships."

To my past teachers, instructors, and employers, "I am not your prodigy. I am completely and utterly myself, with no destination the same as yours. I want to thank you for connecting me with opportunities that allowed me to become better. I think many of you know that the school system is broken for the day and age we live in. Some of the most important information I learned was not during my time in school.

I hope only happiness for all of you and I hope you fight to teach students and employees what is important. There were a few of you that motivated me to do something great and I am forever grateful. What I have found to be more important than the knowledge given to me are the relationships. I was never good at school but always excelled in the jobs that I had, that was not you but simply my own abilities and interests."

"My dearest Ella, your ghost is now gone from my mind, but you are not forgotten. At times I still listen to the same music we played during our long drives. I do this not solely because of you, but rather because it takes me to a more simple and blissful time in my life. I have changed, as I know you have, and I am truly curious in what ways. I do believe that we will meet again, but you will be a different person to which I will not recognize. But how will our personalities compare to each other? You are with him now and I hope he treats you well and with respect. Truthfully I am not sure what I consider respect anymore. I respect others, but now there will always be a piece of me that wants to punish them for the mistakes you and I once made.

You believed that you weren't good at gift-giving. But I am still thankful for the framed picture of us together at the baseball stadium, it continues to be my favorite.

I once wondered if you thought of me when you saw the places we visited together. I now understand that you will never forget me, or forget the memories we shared. I am not who I once was, and I know you are not either. I no longer see you as a princess. You are simply a stranger who happens to share memories with me.

We were never perfect, but you were the closest I had to true love. I do not regret a single memory of ours, every moment you and I shared has made me who I am. You deserve happiness, not from others but from yourself. I have found happiness in myself and now I know how to say how I truly feel. I will never forget the privilege it was to be yours in the two years time we shared. You are not a mistake, you never will be. You are a lesson that I had to learn to find my true self, my happiness. I would never change a single moment, the happiness of those moments will live alongside me for the rest of my life. I was lost, left to myself in that very parking lot I now despise. I was not lost without you but rather lost in the heat of you leaving. I am no longer trapped by the anger that paralyzed my body from leaving that parking lot.

Now here I stand in thanks for every adventure we spent together. Thank you Ella Dallas West, for the memories, for the experience. I have finally realized that my hatred only kept me from my happiness. You are not only a memory but a part of my past. The same part that pushed me to move forward. I forgive you and appreciate who you helped me to become, I only hope you forgive me for my actions and tribulations."

Just as pictures on a television, the memories that flashed in my mind fluttered into a bright blur. As each moment passed, the blur began to clarify into shapes, then objects. I looked around the scholarly decorated room before setting my eyes on a familiar face. My disorientation began to clarify and I realized where I was and who the familiar face was that sat before me in a dark stitched leather chair. It was Dr. Kristian Steele, a therapist I visited monthly for the past year. "Desmond, are you alright, you look pale?" she voiced, jittering with concern. "Yes, I'm okay. Actually, I think I am great." I said in response to her uncertainty. The confusion had completely faded as she looked at me in approval. "Well Desmond, I am very pleased. This is truly one of my favorite stories. I can easily see that you have made significant progress. As long as you agree, I believe this should be our last session." She advised with clear satisfaction.

I quickly jumped to my feet and paced toward the window that overlooked a beautiful Seattle cityscape. I let out a puff of warm air that fogged the glass, as it cleared I began to see my near future. As I refocused my attention to Dr. Steele I advanced, "Thanks for everything Doc."

Notes From the Author

I would like to acknowledge and thank every member of my team and those who helped me to release this book. I also wish to thank anyone who has taken the time to read my book. I have worked diligently and hope that you enjoyed the book. I publish this book with the purpose that people enjoy it and find it to be helpful in their personal growth. All of the photos in this book were taken by myself with the help of my team.

Author & Photographer- Brenden Horned

Chief Editor- Kris Swoboda

Proofreader- Jessa Keller

Character Models- Peyton Still, Destiny Blackburn, and Emilie Barrera